Dedication

For my fourth novel, I dedicate it to all the "Awkward Black Girls". Yes, a shout out to Issa Rae's web series which I so loved! This book deals with a heroine who doesn't fit the conventional mold, even of the current times. I could be considered the same myself! Never extra girly, yet not a tomboy. Social sometimes, but I often prefer my house and my pets. The world can be so "black or white" and those of us in the "gray" areas have to fight to feel comfortable in their *truth*. This book is for women who fall in that non-defined space while they are just trying to live life on their own terms!

"Instant Chemistry Series"

One Click

For

Love

Taylor Love

Taylor Made Day Dreams
Bringing an "imaginative break" to your day!

One Click For Love

ISBN: 978-1-948383-07-3

Taylor Made Daydreams
Westland, MI 48185

www.TaylorMadeDaydreams.com

Cover Credit-Entire Instant Chemistry *Novel* Series-GermanCreative

Proof Reader: L. Parker

Prologue

Brihanna, had stopped in for her once a month dinner at Robert's house. It used to be every two weeks, but when he entered a serious relationship and then got married, their routine changed. The rule was if Robert cooked, they cleaned. Which was pretty much always. Her brother had married the only other black woman over 25 that didn't know how to cook, the other being herself. She had helped his wife Mika clean up, and now was opening her laptop at the kitchen island.

Their shared lack of cooking skills, was one of the things she liked about her new sister-in-law of barely six months. Now her aunt had someone else to fuss at, not that Mika cared. The woman smiled, nodded and waved away the lectures and everyone let her be. Meanwhile, she still got the evil eye from her aunt and the sad head shake from her mother. Apparently, if you had a husband or man you were allowed flaws. If you didn't, you became a "sham" of a woman. Life was not fair to the female gender, even in today's society.

"What are you doing over there that has you sighing like that?" Mika asked, wiping her hands on a dish towel before coming to lean over her guest.

"Nothing, just putting in another hour of work."

"Not on my watch. You are too young to be in this house working on a Saturday."

Brihanna wasn't fooled and narrowed her eyes in the other woman's direction.

"I'm only two years younger than you. Did my mother and aunt put you up to this?"

"Of course not!"

Mika instilled some outrage in her voice. Her mother-in-law *had* asked her to pull her only daughter out of her shell. Though Mika didn't agree she was in one. Brihanna was just a little *different*. A little boring for someone her age but everyone couldn't be the life of the party like herself.

"I'm insulted you think I could be swayed to their camp. I don't want you to get a husband or even a boyfriend. I just want you to get laid."

"What!" Brihanna whipped her head from side to side trying to make sure her brother wasn't around. "Shut up before he hears you!"

"Why does it matter? He's not against sex." Mika grinned knowingly. "Trust me on that."

She planned to jump her husband as soon as his sister left, another great reason to get the woman out the door.

"Come on, are you dating anyone?" Mika sat next to her. "You can tell me." Brihanna shook her head, knowing it was hard to shake Mika when she was on a roll.

"I haven't had a date in two months. But it's cool. I'm not the type of woman that needs a man to define her."

"Umm hmm." Mika rolled her eyes. "Again, he doesn't need to define you, he just needs to break you off. If he's *real* good, make a monthly appointment."

"Robert, your wife is getting on my nerves!" Brihanna yelled into the other room.

Robert heard his sister but ignored her. His name was Robert, not Bennet and he wasn't in it.

"Wait a damn minute. I don't need to be *defined* by a man either. So that should have been, 'Robert, my *sister-in-law* is getting on my nerves'. Get it right."

"Whatever." Brihanna mumbled, turning back to the computer screen.

Mika almost let a full minute go by in silence before snatching the computer away from Brihanna.

"Hey!"

"Calm down. I'm just going to pull up a dating site or two. I'm sure we can find you a date in no time."

"Give it back!"

They tousled over the device, like two fourteen-year olds over a diary. Finally, when both of them were out of breath Brihanna reclaimed her property.

"*You* are crazy. And for your information. I've been on a new dating site, that's where I found the last guy."

"Why didn't you say that?" Mika huffed out. "Pull it up."

Brihanna did, opening her profile on Nerd Passions. Letting Mika spend a few minutes looking over her profile and the messages sent her way.

"Well, I can see why you might not be getting the cream of the crop, why is your profile so militant?"

"It's not. I'm just letting everyone know up front I'm not for the bullshit."

"I see, and that's scaring them away. They're looking for a good time, not a lecture on how shitty they really are." Mika sighed, then softly asked. "Will you please let me redo your profile?"

Brihanna slid the laptop over, after all what did she have to lose? Mika got to work and spent the next twenty minutes changing the profile. Softening the language and other parts she outright deleted. Once she was satisfied, the page was published and the two waited to see what men it would reel in.

"You used one of the wedding photos." Brihanna remarked, looking at the updates. "I look extra girly."

"Yeah, that was the point. Not to mention you look beautiful."

Brihanna couldn't argue that. In the picture she was twirling on the beach, two hours and five drinks after the ceremony. Dusk had started to seep in, while the posted lanterns threw off soft light and the soulful music had given everybody life. It was a great picture. She looked happy, relaxed and carefree.

"My hair is shorter now."

"I know, but I made sure to add more recent photos too. Are you getting hits yet?"

"Yeah, a few actually."

Both women leaned in close so they could read. Brihanna had several men in her inbox already of a variety of races. One caught her eye, and Brihanna spent several minutes reading his profile. Mika noticed and started grinning at her.

"Do we have a winner?" Mika asked wiggling in her seat, already excited.

"I think we do." Brihanna murmured. Going back in the message panel to click the reply button.

Chapter One

Ugh, why in the world had she listened to Mika? Deep down she knew better. She had agreed to meet a man named Lawrence for coffee...tonight. Mika pushed Brihanna to wear one of her multi-colored handkerchief hemmed tops, over her jeans instead of the tee-shirt she'd worn to the house. While it was fairly warm in this last week of May, Brihanna still wore her short leather jacket. The days may have been comfortable, but it was still spring and the nights got cool fast.

Now she was driving to a coffee shop not far from her brother's house as eight-thirty rolled in. It wasn't that she hadn't dated off the internet before, just usually not this quickly. She preferred to chat for a while online or text a few days before meeting. What would they talk about? At this point neither knew anything but what was on the profiles. Brihanna wasn't the best at small talk with complete strangers.

Lawrence's page said he was twenty-nine with no kids, (though she planned to confirm that) and worked in IT. The man shared the same rich brown complexion she did. His face held the slightest touch of roundness until he smiled, then his jawline sharpened his features. Making him favor Michael B. Jordan in *Creed*, haircut and all. He had that cute, nice guy next door look until he hit you with that sexy curve of his lips. Why men rarely smiled in pictures she would never understand. That single look conveyed he had more depth to him. Secrets maybe, along with a hidden side for fun.

Mika had estimated with her eagle eye, that he was about seven inches taller than her 5'5". While he didn't bare his body in the photos, she had been able to tell he was in decent shape and well put together. Brihanna just hoped he wasn't extra boring, or extra technical. Men who were in computer fields didn't understand that she didn't want to hear that shit on dates, she heard and spoke it *every* day at work.

Blowing out a breath that feathered her bangs while parking, she was about to find out either way—assuming she got out the car. To stall, she opened the small clutch bag Mika insisted she take. Brihanna didn't often carry a purse. She didn't have anything against them, but usually carried her keys or clipped them to her jeans, her phone going in a pocket. Most things were paid with the Apple Pay app from her phone, so she didn't have a need for purses often.

Mika had packed her a "date bag" anyway. Opening it, she sorted through the contents. There was a flat pack of tissues, an unopened tube of brown lip gloss, a small bottle of hand lotion plus a compact mirror. Surprised at the practical items, Brihanna smiled, until she dug further down. Uncovering feminine wipes, a couple of condoms, and one of those little tube samples of massage oil! Her sister-in law had tried to be considerate to a potential partner, giving one regular size condom and a magnum. Why Mika had two sizes when she was married to one man was a question for another day. Though Brihanna could guess the answer. Neither Robert nor Mika had been saints before marrying.

Somehow, a hot pink lipstick shaped tube of pepper spray was squeezed in as well. Did Mika expect her to be ravished, kidnapped or both? Laughing, she zipped up the purse exiting the car. Brihanna appreciated the thought behind *all* the items. It was nice to be cared for, even if she could take care of herself. For the first time she had a female family member near her age, two counting Andrea. Except for the pepper spray, none of her male members would have thought to give her these things. Well Darrell *might* have given her some condoms.

Opening the door to the coffee shop, she glanced around. Lawrence said he would be wearing a navy flat cap. Thankfully, he was easy to spot, pairing the cap with a light blue dress shirt. Brihanna reminded herself to be open. Just because he looked like he was going to work didn't mean he'd be dull. Righting the smile on her face, she stepped forward. He looked up from his phone, noticed her and waved, standing as she closed the distance between them.

"Lawrence?"

"Yeah, that's me and you're Brihanna, it's good to meet you."

He leaned forward for a hug at the same time she held out a hand. They both frowned before Lawrence completed the handshake and offered her a seat. Brihanna's hope of a good evening was fading. They weren't even on the same page about how to greet each other.

*

Lawrence hadn't been sure if his date was going to actually show up. Not because she was three minutes late, more so because these dating sites were unpredictable. Half the people were insecure *and* indirect. Her level of directness was one of the things he'd liked about her profile. He wanted someone who would say if they were interested or *not* before wasting tons of time. He didn't mind giving people a try, but he also knew how to call it quits if it wasn't working.

He was glad to see the Brihanna online seemed to be the same person face to face, appearance wise at least. Take tonight for instance, he liked women who knew how to keep it simple unless the occasion called for it. She wore no heavy make-up, only sporting lipstick and a bright pop of eyeshadow. The latter made her doe like eyes pop out even more. He hadn't known if the picture with shorter hair was recent or not. Now he could see that it was. Lawrence liked the longish pixie cut on her. It shaped her oval face nicely, making a person focus on her features.

Personality wise, he was re-judging her. Most women on these dates were more than fine with a hug in greeting. Lawrence had just gotten serious about using these sites to find a more long term partner and not a hookup. If a woman was *only* thinking of sleeping with a guy, she wouldn't be shy about giving a hug at first sight. So Brihanna's preference for a handshake was actually a plus.

"I'm glad you made it."

"Thanks. Sorry I was a little late. You didn't have to wait for me to order."

She had already decided to get one drink and a pastry. Both things could be consumed quickly or slowly depending on if she wanted to leave.

"Sure I did." Lawrence said easily. "Didn't want to be rude, besides I wasn't in a rush."

After they came back from getting their items, he asked the first question of the night.

"I know some people don't like nicknames, but do you mind if I call you Bri?"

"No, not at all."

And she really didn't, almost preferring it. Her cousins, friends and close co-workers called her by the nick name. Only Aunt Dolores, Robert and her mother used her government name.

"What about you? Though I can't think of anything off hand with your first name."

"Some people at work call me Law."

"Really?" Brihanna grinned at that. "Just to shorten Lawrence or is there a story behind it?"

"They claim in my department what I say is the *law*."

She was amused to see the disconcerted look on his face.

"Ahh, so you crack the whip so to speak on your team? I wouldn't have taken you for a hard-ass."

Lawrence chuckled shaking his head in the negative.

"I'm not...most of the time. It's just my job gets a little intense. When the system goes down or some department's service mysteriously goes out, employees really don't care about why, they just want it fixed. In turn I have to push my team to diagnose it and correct it *quickly*."

"Got it. I totally get people being shitty when they're going through internet or document withdrawal."

"That's putting it mildly. They're pissed from the first moment the issue starts."

"Now I feel bad. I work from home fairly often. I'll have to go easy on our IT team next time our VPN isn't working""

"Look at that, I'm making life better for IT workers one person at a time."

They shared a chuckle before Brihanna got serious.

"Your profile said you don't have any kids, no wife or girlfriend...is that correct?"

"Yep, and it's the truth."

Lawrence wasn't offended by the questions, thought it was smart of her to ask. Anyone could say anything online, but most people usually gave something away when they had to lie to your face.

"Have you been on this site long or met a lot of folks from it?"

"No, only a few months. You're the second person I've met directly." Brihanna pointed out. "Honestly, dating is normally not at the top of my to-do list. I don't even check my hits often."

"What put you on the lookout for company tonight?"

Pressing her lips together she considered what to say. Should she tell him her family thought she was one step removed from being a modern-day spinster? That she'd been hustled by an expert to go on this date tonight? While she didn't embarrass easily, even she thought that sounded a little pathetic.

"Umm, I was bored and decided to check in...then you reached out."

"Ahh, my timing was lucky. I'll take it. I've told you what I do, what's your nine-to-five? Your profile mentioned you're a programmer, of what exactly?"

"I program video games." She answered, knowing what was coming next.

"No shit? Anything I might know?"

Naming a popular fantasy game that most people knew of, made his eyebrows rise.

"That's what's up. You continue to get more and more interesting." Lawrence gave her a pleased grin. "I'm *very* happy you came out."

Chapter Two

They talked about several games both enjoyed, also finding out they liked comics. Making them both certified black nerds, or Blerds for short. The conversation was flowing and fairly relaxed. It was nowhere near as awkward as she envisioned. Brihanna found him easy to talk to and not as buttoned up as she'd originally taken him for. All of this should have put her completely at ease, instead it had the opposite effect. What was wrong with him that he needed a dating site? He seemed personable enough, smart and he had a good job. He was also pretty damn cute. Instead of wondering about it she decided to ask.

"Throwing one of your earlier questions back at you. How often do you use dating sites?"

"In the last year, not that often." He gave her an unconcerned smile. "I'm only on one other right now. I check both maybe once or twice a month."

"When was the last time you dated someone before tonight?"

"A month ago, and before you ask it was a one date thing and I didn't sleep with her. We didn't hit it off."

"Still sounds better than the guy I met." Brihanna sat back, thinking on that disaster. "Basically, he wanted to practice his *dating a black person skills*. But I wasn't interested in being his swirl experiment. After asking a few questions I found out he had a real crush on this black lady at his job, but felt uneasy about asking her out."

Amused, Lawrence took another sip of his coffee.

"Did you give him any advice before you booted him?"

"I was in a decent mood so yes. He was so pathetic it was kinda sweet. I just told him to man up. That a woman was a woman. Brown, black, white, whatever."

"This is true. Does that mean you're pretty open about who you date?"

"Why not? I try to keep an open mind about a lot of things."

"I like the sound of that." And he really did. Any woman that was going to keep him interested would need to be. "I'll have to remember that for the future."

"Don't think too far ahead." Glancing down at her phone, she bit her lip. "In fact, it's getting late. I think I should be heading home."

Brihanna pulled a few bills out, holding them across the table to Lawrence. The man looked at her as if she had manifested a second head.

"What's that for?"

"My portion you paid."

"Key word is paid for, as in done, over. You don't need to pay me back."

"But I want to...considering." She waved the money back and forth.

"What exactly are you *considering* Bri?"Lawrence leaned back, resisting the urge to cross his arms.

She heard the hint of sarcasm in his voice and twisted her own lips in an ironic smile, finally letting her arm drop.

"That this is a "meet up". I don't want to seem like I'm taking advantage, since I'm calling it a night and going home *alone*."

"Wait so you think, *I* think you owe me sex? Because I paid ten dollars for a drink and a scone." He chuckled. "Gotta say that's a new one."

Brihanna didn't think it was that farfetched.

"I figured this might rank in your mind a blow-job at least. And I'm fresh out of those for the month."

Lawrence laughed even harder. "Really? What would I have been expecting if I paid for a full meal?"

"I don't know. You tell me."

Losing the mirth, Lawrence leaned forward.

"Nothing. I'm into *a lot* of things, but paying for sex isn't one of them. I use the sites for dates mostly, someone to chill with and have a good time." He shrugged. "Have I had sex with dates in the past? Yes, when everyone was down for the cause. I haven't used them much lately as I'm tired of all the hookups. While I won't lie and say I'm looking for something ultra-serious, I *am* looking for something more long term than the one-night stand zone. Believe it or not, not all men want to be on-demand studs."

"Gotta say I do find that hard to believe." Bri flung his earlier sarcasm back his way. "Are you telling me if I said I wanted to get down right now, you'd say no?"

Lawrence took his time appraising her, letting his eyes linger on her lips and chest before locking eyes with her again.

"Are you saying that's what you want?"

Hearing his voice drop to that tone of seduction men had, threw her off guard. Causing Brihanna to take longer than normal to answer, "No."

"Then I have no answer for that hypothetical question. What I *do* know, is that the bill is paid. Why don't you let it stay that way?"

Brihanna stared a little longer before slowly sliding her arm back across the table.

"Fine. If we ever go out again the next one is on me."

Lawrence watched as she returned the money to her pocket, while he tried to clear her bluff of a question from his mind. Would he have been down for sleeping with her even if it was a one-night stand? No point in mulling it over, so he moved on.

"Okay, last question of the night Bri. What's your thoughts on wanting another date? Be honest, games are a waste of our time."

"I can appreciate that. Right now, I'd have to say *maybe*, no games involved. I'm just not sure how I feel about the night or you yet. To be fair I have a bad habit of over analyzing stuff, but well that's my truth."

He stared at her intently before nodding his head.

"I actually understand, I have the same habit. Tell you what, I'll leave it up to you. Contact me within the next couple of weeks. If I don't hear from you...I'll take the hint."

"Sounds good." Brihanna stood up and he did the same. "I did enjoy our conversation Lawrence."

"Me too, let me walk you out."

"Oh, I don't need you to do that."

"You may not need it, but I want to. Besides, my car is in the parking lot just like yours."

Refusing to feel stupid by his logic, she walked out. Okay, he was a stubborn one. Brihanna made sure her car key was sticking out between the fingers of her balled fist. Though really, he would be the stupidest rapist if he attacked her outside a well-lit Starbucks, in Royal Oak no less. But her mama, aunt, brother and cousins didn't raise no fool. Overly cautious was better than unprepared. It didn't take them long before they reached her Kia Niro and she gave her good-byes.

"Thanks again, for getting me out the house tonight."

"Same here." He tilted his head in her direction. "Drive safe Bri. I hope to hear from you soon."

Chapter Three

Brihanna was bored, and even worse she was horny. Damn, but her PMS made her feel freaky. Normally she ignored it, or took care of it quickly and got on with life. But she'd been feeling the "itch" for a few days now, and on this fine second Saturday in June she wanted someone else to "scratch" it. Naughty thoughts weighing so heavily on her mind, she had cancelled dinner at her brothers already. Instead, she was sitting at home wondering how to solve this problem.

Annoyingly her mind went straight to Lawrence. Two weeks since their coffee date and she still didn't know what she thought of the man. She was feeling a tad paradoxical about him. She either liked people right away or didn't. Rarely did she have an in between feeling for someone. But with Mr. Lawrence "Law" Townsend she'd ran into a problem. Brihanna could tell he was more than what he seemed, and that intrigued her.

Maybe they were only meant to be friends. Which made it awkward that she was thinking of calling and asking him to *help a sista out*. The man said he wasn't interested in being used as a *stud*, which made her wonder was he exaggerating or *not* with the term. Hell he was a guy, probably running that "I'm looking for more than a booty call, less than a relationship" game anyway. And even if he wasn't, what man would turn down some no strings attached loving when offered?

None that she knew of.

The term "friend with benefits" had been made just for situations like this. A couple of days after meeting, she sent him a message through the dating site. A lame, "It was good meeting you," message. He'd sent something just as generic back, but that had started the communication going at least. Since then they chatted almost every day. He would randomly send her corny computer jokes, made more so because she understood them. Then just this Monday Lawrence sent her his phone number, with a quick message only saying, "if you ever want to talk live". Brihanna respected that he'd left it at that, hadn't pushed.

She hadn't called yet, still unsure if she wanted him to have her number. But she admitted she had enjoyed getting to know him better. Learning about their shared and different interests made her believe she would enjoy hanging out with him in a more laid-back setting. *This* led her to think he might be a decent guy, which helped her reach the conclusion Lawrence might be a good option to meet her current sexual needs. As always, she'd over thought it.

Sitting here now she *really* wanted that itch scratched, rubbed, grabbed, and pounded—hell, whatever he was into. With those adjectives rattling around in her brain, she picked up the phone scrolling down to his name. When she had stored the number, part of her knew she would eventually use it, just not for this. Damn her energetic hormones for moving up the timetable!

*

Lawrence was at home Saturday evening straight chilling. He deserved it after having a long irritating week. Which started with a system crash at the main office on a damn Monday. On Wednesday, he'd gone over to the second site to oversee some network upgrades. By the time Friday rolled around he'd totally forgot that it was his birthday weekend. If it hadn't been for his employees bringing in a cake and getting him a card, he would have forgotten.

He had good-naturedly gotten through the office celebration, when what he really wanted to do was get the hell away from people, which was a no-go as he'd also forgotten he was meeting friends after work. Not wanting to cancel, he had shown up and was having fun until an unwanted thought entered his mind.

———

He and the guys were having a meal and a couple of drinks at CJ Mahoney's, talking crap and half-way watching sports.

"Man, you about to be old." Jarod a friend from college announced loudly.

"I'm turning thirty not fifty-five."

"Shit man, fifty-five isn't old." Jerome a previous supervisor and close friend from his very first job chimed in. "Anyway, thirty is a golden age. Live that shit up. Women aren't the only ones that start going downhill at forty."

Lawrence laughed, shaking his head. "And you know from experience? You're only forty-two."

"And what's wrong with a woman in her forties?" Malcolm his cousin interjected. "Hell, I like my women nice and seasoned."

"I was just talking mess," Jerome said. "My wife is sexy as hell, just turned the big 4-0 last year. Women seem to come into their own around that time or something. She's been freaky as all get out lately."

"I'm going to tell her you said that, the next time I see her." Lawrence threatened.

"But since we on the subject of freaky." Lawrence's other cousin Mike spoke up. "You got some birthday booty lined up, or what?"

"Nope." Lawrence took another long pull from his first bottle of beer.

"You have another day to rectify that. Or handle it tonight. Right over there we have several fine ladies to choose from. Take your shot."

Lawrence knew exactly who Mike was talking about. A group of women had been chattering at a table nearby. Lots of laughter, drinks and peeks over at his table since the guys had sat down. Maybe he should take his cousin's advice. After the week he'd had a release would be welcome. It had been too damn long since he'd had some anyway.

"Maybe." he said out loud.

The table started giving their opinion on who to focus on, he ignored them, taking his own assessment. The four women certainly offered up enough variety for any man to choose from. There was a cute, white chick and a curvy senorita with hair down to her ass, that he could see wrapping around his fist. Then two pretty sisters of different shades of brown, rounded out the table, one of which had been eyeballing him all night. As he was running his eyes over her body, she caught him. Flicking out her tongue then explicitly licking her lips in clear invitation. It was so blatant everyone at both tables saw it—and like that he lost interest.

Lawrence had learned that often the ones who were the most sexually aggressive from the start, couldn't handle what he wanted. They could talk the talk, but not walk the walk. And out of nowhere Brihanna flashed to his mind. She had a good amount of directness to her, without coming off jaded, not to mention a wide stripe of practicality. He liked that she thought things out, an indication that she was all in after making decisions. Ignoring the invitation from the hottie across the room, Lawrence focused back on his friends.

"I'm straight on the women tonight. I just want one more drink and to watch this sorry excuse of a Pistons game."

—

Lawrence never did much for his birthdays anyway, and it looked like this year would be the same. Waking early on Saturday to take calls from his mom and other various family, before acknowledging all the online well wishes throughout the rest of the day. He was finally relaxing as evening rolled in. This left his mind wide open, and wouldn't you know it brought him back to thinking about pretty little Bri.

She was still a little standoffish, though he'd seen peaks of her lighter side as they talked back and forth. So maybe he just needed to accept that she had "friend zoned" him. He'd thrown her a feeler out in the form of his phone number Monday and got nothing back. That had been the cap on that particular shitty day. When it was all said and done if she didn't want to take it further, then that was that. Being only friends with a woman wasn't a problem for him. He had a number of them at work and occasionally hung out with a few in groups.

Bri was surprisingly mature for her age, then again women had the jump on men in that area. With her, he could easily see them being computer pals. She was witty and intelligent, so at least he could be assured of interesting conversations. Lawrence didn't fool himself, he could now answer that "hypothetical" question. If she'd been willing, he would love to see if he could make her melt in his hands. Too damn bad birthday wishes didn't come true, otherwise he knew what *his* would be.

When the phone rang, he gave it a casual glance. Normally he wouldn't pick up an unknown number. But with the way people changed phones at a drop of a hat, he figured it might be another person he knew saying happy birthday.

"It's Law." He heard a few seconds of silence, before hearing the voice he wasn't expecting.

"Hey, it's Bri."

Lawrence came to attention. "What's up?"

"Not much. I was wondering if you're busy? I was looking to get into something tonight."

If ever there was a time she should be blunt, Brihanna thought it was now. Seeing as how she wanted him to get into *her*. Instead of saying so, she was trying to use some of that "tack" her mother often said she lacked.

Brihanna had Lawrence's full attention. He figured if she just wanted to hang out, she would have messaged him like usual. He considered himself good at hearing, and reading between the lines, and this definitely was screaming "hookup". But he preferred to be sure about these things.

"Oh really? What *exactly* do you have in mind Bri?"

She sighed, stifling her annoyance at not going with her first instinct.

"I'm looking to hang out, *and* hookup." There it was.

"I see..." Lawrence said slowly.

Brihanna didn't.

Her libido needed answers. Was he interested? Offended? It had never occurred to her that he'd been thinking of "friend zoning" *her*.

"Look, I know you're a little adverse to just getting it on and what not, but I happen to be in a mood for human-to-human contact. It's okay if you're not interested. You were one of the first persons I thought to reach out to."

"Oh...is there a list?" Lawrence let out a chuckle. "I guess I should be flattered to be at the top."

"I didn't mean it, like it sounded. Though what if I did? You men have a list all the time."

"*I* don't have a list." He responded plainly. "And I wouldn't care if *you* did. I'm all for equal rights in how men and women live their sexual lives."

"Okay then. But just to be clear I don't have a list. This is a rare mood for me. I just meant *if* you're not interested...I could move on and no hard feelings."

"Slow up, I haven't said I'm not interested."

"You haven't said you are either. Or did I just make an *ass*-sumption that you didn't already have other plans tonight? Damn, I'm sorry. My hormone monster has been riding me hard lately."

Lawrence busted out laughing. "You watch 'Big Mouth' too?"

"Yes!" Brihanna was pleased beyond reason that he'd *got it*. "It's a crazy good, but stupid show."

"I agree. Look...I'm open to making an exception for you. You know, help you out. But I'm not going to be a cheap date. You caught me on the wrong day, today's my birthday.

"Looks like I'll be getting you the perfect gift."

"Let's just say that was on my *birthday* list. We'll have to wait to see if it's perfect or not. If I don't get a good date activity I might not put out, so make it good."

"I can do that." Brihanna lowered her own voice. "After all it's your birthday...so it's whatever you want."

"Now that's what I like to hear." That one sentence from her, had him literally getting stiff.

They decided that she would pick him up around 7:30. He quickly texted her his address while they were still on the phone, then saved her number after they hung up. Lawrence was frankly a little stunned, this might be one of the best birthdays he'd had in a while! He had thought for sure he'd struck out with her, now she was serving herself up on a silver platter. Looking around his house, he figured there was only a little straightening up to do. Looked like he was about to get that birthday booty after all.

Chapter Four

It was a good thing that Brihanna didn't have much time to think. Had she just agreed to pay for sex, in the form of taking a man out for a birthday date? Also, if she was being non sexist, men had been doing the same to women since forever. If they both got what they wanted, so be it. Frankly, there was more excitement than shame in her game at the moment. Since time was short, she spent the next thirty minutes finding something to do located by his house. And it had to be close, because afterwards they were heading straight to a bed.

Once that was done she had to get herself together. She didn't have that much time as he lived in Troy, which was a minimum thirty-minute drive. In the shower she prayed he didn't turn out to be a dud. In her decade as an official adult, she'd had one out right bad sexual encounter and it was enough to last her a lifetime. Sex should never be *that* bad. Hell, it wouldn't even take much to get her off right now. All she needed was him to be *decent*. Good would be a plus, but she wasn't holding her breath for great.

When she arrived Brihanna saw that he lived in a nice little neighborhood, in a well-kept Ashmont-brick ranch style home. Running her sweaty hands down her black jeans, Brihanna got out the car. She had on a semi sparkly silver tank top, under a short thin jacket, her compromise on getting dressed up. Topped off with large hoop earrings that had "black girl magic" cut out in the middle. A deep plum lipstick completed the look. She had everything else she would need for the night in a small, silver wrist clutch. Well, except the pair of socks stuffed in her back pocket. Shaking off the light nerves she headed up the drive, barely ringing the doorbell before it opened. Looked like she wasn't the only one excited.

"Hey! You're right on time."

"Hey yourself."

Had he looked this good last time they met? Or were her hormones upping the effect? Maybe it was his cologne, and why was she just noticing the dimple in his left cheek?

Rubbing his hands in anticipation, Lawrence stepped outside.

"I'm ready to see what you have in store."

"Wait." Brihanna tried sticking her head indoors. "I don't get to come inside? What are you hiding? And if you say your mama, I swear I'm out."

Lawrence laughed but firmly closed the door and locked it.

"You're funny, did you know that? Did you forget you'll be seeing the place tonight? I'll be happy to give you a full tour. Either before or after we hit the bedroom."

Brihanna blinked. His mannerisms could be so unassuming she forgot he could be as candid as she was. He often reminded her of Cam or her cousin Darrell with his laid-back vibe, so his directness sometimes caught her off guard.

"Well played." She grudgingly conceded. "Come on before we're late."

She drove them eight miles up the road and parked in the Skate World of Troy lot. When she turned in her seat he was smiling and Brihanna felt better about her choice.

"How do you know I can skate?"

"Come on you're a Detroit boy, I know you can get around the rink at least."

"I should be able to do that much." Lawrence agreed before getting out the car. He could get used to being chauffeured around.

"Don't worry. I'll make sure the birthday boy doesn't get hurt. Remember I have plans for him."

Lawrence marveled at the difference in her, as she paid for the entrance fee and skates. To be fair, he would be disappointed to encounter the same person from their first date, seeing how they'd gotten to know each other better. Her body language and verbal quips were definitely flirty. He liked this different side of her and was eager to see how this progressed. When she grabbed them a locker, storing her small purse and jacket he added his keys. Falling on those would hurt like the devil. Then they were lacing up the old style skates and hitting the floor.

He let her take them around slowly a couple of times, appreciating that it was "old school night" so the music was good at least. Lawrence disciplined his mind to stay in the moment and not think about getting that lean and athletic body of hers under him. Luckily, he was skilled at controlling his body as well. He was looking forward to just enjoying the night. It had been a while since he'd had real fun with a woman.

"You think you're warmed up yet?" Brihanna gave him an encouraging nudge.

"Yeah, I think it's coming back to me." Lawrence executed a smooth move so he could skate backwards, all while speeding up and leaving her behind.

Her mouth dropped open just for a second, before those inquisitive eyes of hers narrowed. When she caught up to him she coasted, crossing her arms in attitude.

"Ooohhh, your little lying behind!"

"I never said I *couldn't* skate."

"Yeah whatever. Showoff." She bumped him with her shoulder as she skated past.

"It's like that huh?" Lawrence said with amusement, righting himself before going after her.

They spent the next ten minutes racing about the rink like kids, trying to outdo each other. Then finally settled down and started skating in synch. They even broke out some moves when a good song came on. Brihanna had forgotten how much she enjoyed roller skating. For an ambivert it had been the perfect activity. Something that once you got into, made you think you were in your own world.

They finally took a break about an hour in, and Brihanna was glad she'd ditched the jacket. Skating made you hot as hell with the quickness! Not only that but she was feeling it in her legs already too. She started rolling to the locker and Lawrence followed.

"I'm about to grab us some waters."

"I can do that." He said automatically.

"No, you sit, remember this is your date. I need to keep you hydrated."

Lawrence laughed appreciating the naughty smirk she tossed his way. He had to say he loved that she was a little dirty minded, but not in a practiced way. When Brihanna came back, she not only had waters but was somehow balancing fries and chicken fingers. They dug in, teasing and laughing, ignoring everything around them but each other. Finished, he suggested they play pool in the game area and Brihanna reluctantly agreed.

"I don't know. I hate to lose and I'm not that good."

"I'll go easy on you, even teach you a few tips." Lawrence assured her. "I'll even let you break first."

Brihanna nodded, watching him rake the balls. When she went to break her stick fumbled a bit, and while she connected the balls barely scattered, much less went into a hole.

"You weren't kidding, huh?" Lawrence shook his head. "Look, in the spirit of being kind on my birthday, why don't we start over and I'll show you a better way to break?"

Brihanna shrugged. "I'm not going to complain about you making my chances of winning better."

After he set up again, he demonstrated how to hold the pool stick, how to maneuver it forward with some power behind it. When she tried to duplicate it, he only shook his head harder.

"No, let me show you."

He came behind her pretty close, putting his hands and arms over hers to position them. The feel of his skin on hers made her shiver. He must have felt a zap too because he stiffened, before his hands relaxed. Then he was stroking down her forearms instead of merely holding them, coming closer so his front was flush against her backside.

"See what you have to do is grab the stick firmly, with your fingers like this."

His voice was definitely sounding rough against her ear and she shivered again.

"Okay." And damned if hers wasn't coming out low and soft.

"Then you lean over." He bent her forward against the table, which naturally pressed her ass against his crotch.

Brihanna swallowed, her throat suddenly dry. It had been a minute, but she still recognized a firm penis when she felt one. It *had* to be the PMS making her so sensitive to his touch.

"Are you cold?" Lawrence purposely let his tongue flick the bottom of her earlobe.

Brihanna had barely resisted jumping at the touch, but she couldn't help her answer from coming out on a near moan.

"No, the exact opposite."

"Hmmm, now where was I? So then you want to square it up. Let the stick go in...and out. In and out of the hole your fingers created a couple of times."

"That sounds good...I mean like a good idea."

"Mmm hmm, it is good, it's very good. Then when you think you've found just the *right* spot, you push forward hard."

He demonstrated with the stick *and* his hips.

Somehow, she kept a sound of surprise from escaping. They stayed pressed together as they watched balls scatter across the table, one going in the far corner pocket. Was she subtly wiggling her behind against him, why yes she was! Brihanna might have done more if it wasn't for some loud teenagers coming in, reminding her they were in full view of the public. Suddenly turning to face him, they stared at each other. Well, at each other's lips at least.

"See how that worked?" Lawrence cleared his throat. "You got solids. You just need a firm grip on the stick so you can control it."

"I'll remember that. Thanks for the tip."

"Anytime Bri."

Lawrence walked around the table, rearranging the bulge in his pants as he went. This woman had him about to make a damn fool of himself. What had happened to his control? Another couple of minutes and he was sure someone would've had cause to call the police for lewd behavior. He was barely paying attention as she took her next turn, still thinking about how perfectly he fit against her ass. Even through layers of clothes, her flesh had been soft, and that sent his mind wondering what it was going to feel like naked. Just the thought had his mouth watering.

It was no wonder he didn't zone back in until she had taken and made her second shot on her own. Now he watched a little stupefied as she expertly held her stick and proceeded to knock another two balls in.

"I thought you said you weren't that good at pool?"

"Did I say that?" Brihanna lined up her next shot. Locking eyes with him, she sunk the ball without looking. "Maybe its beginner's luck."

"Luck my ass." He muttered, getting out of her way as she made next shot.
"Why did you sit there and let me help you?"

"Left side corner pocket." Brihanna called out her plans for the 8 ball before continuing.

"Maybe because I liked *your* instruction." She took the shot and it went in nice and easy. "That's game."

"I'll remember you said that. More importantly *you* remember it." He gave her a serious look before laughing. "I'm over here playing with a pool shark. Best out of five?"

"Okay." She sweetly agreed.

She still won. Three to two before they moved on to play ski ball, where both won three games. They were fine with leaving it at that.

"Good game." Brihanna gave him a light pat on the back. "We seem well matched."

"I agree." He turned bringing them toe to toe but didn't touch her. "I've had fun, but I'm done playing games for the night. I'm ready to go see if we're well matched in other areas...are you?"

Around the tightness in her throat she managed to get out a coherent, "Yep." It looked like the X-rated games were about to begin.

Chapter Five

The drive back to his house went by in a blur. She deftly took part in the conversation while inside her mind could only think about one thing—bed, her and him. Okay, so make that three things. She cautioned herself to tamper down her expectations. Things had gone well so far and there seemed to be some real chemistry going on. But Brihanna knew sometimes things took a dive once a couple got naked. For some reason she *really* didn't want to be disappointed tonight.

Lawrence had a habit of assessing things in depth before forming a conclusion, but not tonight. He didn't need a long time to figure out they were both primed for what was about to happen. Their overall vibe had him fascinated. The car literally vibrated with sexual energy. Excitement from them both, a tiny level of nervousness from her, and a big helping of outright lust coming from his direction. Lawrence had no clue how it would all end, but couldn't wait to find out.

Traffic was even lighter than before. Troy wasn't a party city, more geared towards business, so most people were off the streets as they reached his house around 11:30. Pulling into the driveway illuminated by solar lights, they unbuckled their seat belts once the car was off. Brihanna was reaching for her door when she noticed he wasn't moving

"Is there a problem?" She asked.

"Not at all. Patiently waiting until you let me out."

"Really?" She went to laugh then saw he was serious.

"Come on, you've been such a *gentlewoman* so far." Lawrence teased. "Don't ruin it now because you're in a rush to get my pants off."

"You..." Brihanna sputtered before snapping her mouth shut.

She wasn't sure if a cuss word or a laugh would escape, so she firmed her lips against both. Either way, she had to be a bit petty by taking her time letting him out.

"After you." Brihanna swept her hand towards the walkway. Following him, then blocking the door with her body at the last minute.

"I thought you said games were over."

"Yeah, *those* games." Lawrence sent her a sly smile. "Now are you going to let me open the door, so we can play the new games I have in mind?"

"I'm not stopping you." Brihanna asserted.

She *so* wanted him to touch her again. Looking her dead in the eye he leaned in close. Reaching around her body to open the door, somehow not touching her at all. Once inside he steered her through the kitchen to the living area.

Taking a slow turn, she looked around. There was one low light on and Lawrence didn't move to turn on more. The room was laid out sparingly but well put together and nice. He seemed to be *very* orderly, which was a departure from the other men whose homes she'd visited. He also had a normal sized TV of about 32" instead of the monstrosity most guys had these days.

"Nice place, and no mother unless you have her tied up in the basement."

Lawrence snickered shaking his head before walking forward.

"I have lots of things in my basement...but a mother isn't one of them. Do you want to see?"

She had helped close the distance as well and now she reached out, lightly grabbing onto his t-shirt.

"Maybe another time, unless you also have a bed down there."

His laughing eyes became thoughtful. "Bri, do you think you're ready to give me what I want?"

"Yeah, I'm ready."

"I'll be the final judge of that."

"Tell me what you want, and I'll give it to you." Brihanna offered in what she hoped passed for a suggestive tone.

Sometimes, she *felt* like a fool when she called herself being flirtatious. Lawrence stepped back breaking the connection, walking around her until he was able to fall into the black easy-chair.

"Strip for me."

"What now?"

"You heard me Brihanna." He quietly admonished.

Her full name had her blinking, and her shoulders squaring. She'd never done a strip tease before. But there was a first time for everything, and her clothes needed to come off anyway.

Sarcastically she inquired, "Do you want me to dance too?"

"Not unless you want to." When she still hesitated, he picked up a small remote on the table next to him and hit a button. "Here, maybe this will help."

Music suddenly filled the room, but Brihanna didn't flinch. She was still staring at him, cocking her head as the first notes played out. It didn't take her more than a few seconds to recognize the iconic strains of the *Art of Noise: Moments in Love.*

Her lips parted and she finally moved, sliding the clutch strap off her wrist and tossing it to the couch. She'd just learned something about the man by this song choice— mainly that he didn't play fair. If she hadn't been in the mood before, which she totally was, *this* song would have gotten her there fast. Unhurriedly taking off the jacket, sending it to join her purse, Brihanna had no plans to dance, not wanting to chance making a fool of herself.

But this song could make anyone feel sexy and she was no exception. Taking another step closer she unbuttoned her jeans, slid the zipper down but left it at that. Instead she bent, prying off one low-heeled sandal, then the other. Kicking those out the way, she took time to lick her dry lips. Even with the lights low, he could probably see her pulse hammering in her neck. She didn't have much else to take off and made a split-second decision on what would go first.

Brihanna took off her high-necked tank-top, neither fast nor slow, then went to unsnap her plain black bra. With one hook undone she decided against it. Taking another small step towards the silent man watching her every move. She brought her hands to her hips, pushing her tight jeans down to her thighs before pausing. She had a ridiculous urge to laugh nervously but didn't.

To be sure she had a *few* pairs of fancy, sexy underwear sets. But she hadn't seen tonight's bootie call as a romantic encounter and had gone with something more amusing. Hoping they'd be too busy tearing each other's clothes off for him to notice, or at most share a chuckle about it. So she watched his eyes track to her panties, saw the slow predatory smile spread to his lips as he read the words "face down" on the front of her boy-cut undies. But it wasn't enough to make him move.

Maybe this might do the trick. Doing a little shuffle to turn around, she waited a few seconds, then bent at her hips. Making the words on this side of the panties, "ass up" a reality. With her backside only a hands length from his face, she finished tugging off the jeans, straightening up and letting her panties fall to the floor with one good push and wiggle. With her back still facing him, she finished unhooking the bra and flung it in his direction without even looking. She heard it land, and after taking a deep breath turned around.

"Now what?"

Was that her voice sounding breathless and shaky? Damn, but the man hadn't even touched her yet!

"*Now...come undress me.*"

Through her eyes, he saw her intelligent mind race, then she was walking towards him. Lawrence was squeezing her bra in one fist, taking her in from head to toe, while one thought ran through his mind.

Happy fucking birthday to me!

Eyelashes lowered, Brihanna leaned down removing his gray t-shirt efficiently over his head. But after it was gone she took her time letting her hands slide over his smooth skin, passing her fingers through the sparse hair on his chest. She'd taken note of the muscles in his arms tonight, now she was impressed with his chest as well. She was pretty sure he was more ripped than the majority of computer geeks she'd ever met. Delighting in his pecs jerking as she ran her nails across them, she followed her hands down to his waist, slowly sinking to her knees. Not focusing on his jeans, instead moving her hands directly to his feet.

Brihanna loosened the laces of his gray leather Air Force Ones before removing them and his socks. Only then did she glance up again into a pair of eyes that were watching her so intently her breath caught in her lungs. She literally had to remind herself to inhale, so penetrating was his gaze.

Except for the bulge in his pants, and the fire in his eyes that was damn near scalding her, he hadn't given any other indication that he liked what she was doing. But when she loosened his belt, then slid the zipper over his engorged flesh, he suddenly sat forward. She didn't move back, palming him through the denim, squeezing him softly. He dropped her bra so both hands could clench the chair.

His lips parted, letting out a heavy breath. The tremor that ran through his tense body pleased her. Now it was clear he was as turned on as she was. But Lawrence seemed to regain control, firming his lips while lifting his hips. Brihanna took the hint pulling his pants and underwear down and over his firm ass. And then he surprised her by pushing to his feet.

Feeling flushed, she prayed not to blush. Lowering her face just in case, she finished tugging down his clothes, sitting back as he kicked them away. She didn't know what to expect, but it wasn't for him to continue towering over her. Glancing up she finally got a good look at his manhood. *Any* doubt that he didn't want her, was put to rest.

He stood fully at attention, long and proud, his ball sac hanging large below. She was already wet from this unusual foreplay and seeing him now only made her more so. Finally looking at his face, she found him watching her. Did he want a blow job, because hell *she* wanted to suck him off. Raising up on her knees, her fingernails getting a firm hold on his strong thighs, she was about to lick her tongue against his balls when he spoke.

"Brihanna...get up."

His voice carried so much arousal he didn't even sound like the same man. Using his legs as leverage she rose, before her hands went to his hips. Lawrence crossed his arms behind her back, pulling her close. *Finally bringing them skin to skin.* The sensation of electricity that went through her body had her clutching at his back. When Lawrence tilted his head to hers, their lips jumped straight to an open mouth kiss.

It was outstanding, this first meeting of lips and tongues. Brihanna could swear their *need* had a taste, and it was sweet and savory. Within seconds Lawrence somehow took total control, even though he wasn't using his hands he commanded her mouth. Devoured her air, while crushing her hardened nipples to his chest. She didn't know how long they sampled the buffet of each other's mouth. But when he stroked over her ass before squeezing hard, she melted, legs giving clean away.

As if that was the cue he'd been waiting on, he scooped her up. She hadn't expected him to be strong enough to carry her, but apparently he was. Curling into his chest, she held on, her mind too muddled with desire and nerves to think straight. She already felt wrung out and they hadn't even had sex yet! As if he could hear her thoughts, Lawrence whispered in her ear.

"We're just getting started Bri. I have plans for you."

Chapter Six

When they entered the bedroom Lawrence let her slide down his body, luxuriating in the feel of her warm skin. He'd smelled her cotton candy scented lotion all night, but now it almost overwhelmed his senses. He couldn't wait to taste a mouthful of confection! Reaching on the shelf behind him he clicked a few buttons on a second remote, music flowed into the room, while dark blue light lit up the space.

"Damnit, what did I get myself into?" Brihanna mumbled against his chest, sneaking her tongue out to lick him, not expecting the sharp tap on the ass it earned her.

"Behave, and get up on that bed."

Backing up until she could sit, she asked, "It's your party, how do you want me?"

"Face down, ass up. Don't look so shocked, I'm just following the directions you gave me."

Opening her mouth to speak, she thought better of it. Rolling, she climbed further up on the bed, staying on her hands and knees. After a few seconds of hesitation, she lowered to her forearms, her ass naturally lifting.

"Don't get shy now, open those legs for me."

She spread 'em, and damned him for being right. Somehow this felt extremely intimate, made her feel open and exposed, and she wasn't just talking about her body. This was turning her on more than it should. The way he was speaking and just knowing he was looking at her most private place while she couldn't see him, had her wet and ready. No wonder she didn't hear him move, how could she over the thudding heart in her chest. Brihanna felt, more than heard him say "you're beautiful" against the lips of her pussy, before his tongue lashed out.

"Ooohhh weee, yes!"

He licked and sucked her from behind, all in her folds and secret places. Time became a concept only, her mind couldn't tell a minute from an hour as her pleasure mounted, nor did she care. Brihanna only knew it felt *sooo* good, that wet tongue against her heated flesh. She was certain several small orgasms resulted from his talents. At long last she was penetrated—with two of his fingers. They made her whimper out a *"yes, yes"* while her muscles clutched around them. And when Lawrence started to slowly finger fuck her, Brihanna almost cried with relief *and* frustration.

She wanted more, wanted it harder and faster. The man had already kept her waiting too long. But when she pushed back against his hand trying to up the tempo, he pinched her left ass cheek hard, causing her to jerk and let out a yelp. At the same time her body tightened around his hand.

"Behave Baby Girl." Lawrence was already struggling to hold back, the feel and taste of her wasn't making it easy. "Matter of fact, stretch your arms all the way out."

Brihanna turned her head and uttered a "but" which was as far as she got before receiving another pinch. Shivering at the zing it sent along her nerves, she reached her arms forward. This pressed her breasts against the bed and her ass tilted even further up. With her arms now flat against the bed, this position gave her no way to push back.

What it did allow was for him to sink his fingers even deeper, making her moan in delight at the invasion. But still he kept his pace slow and deliberate. It was driving her mad, she was literally soaking wet with need. The angle was hitting all the right places, and before long her legs were shaking.

Her loud breathing joining the chorus of the music. Right when she didn't think she could take it, he gave her more. Adding a third finger and speeding up—then he started thumbing her clit. In under thirty seconds he had her squirming and babbling.

"Law-rence, I need, I ne-"

"What do you need Bri, tell me?"

"I *need* to come!"

He didn't say anything, just continued to stroke in and out, out and in as her body wound tighter and tighter, until finally she heard his deep whisper.

"You can come."

And she did.

The knot of pent up pleasure in her belly came loose and exploded inside her body. She buried her own face in the covers to scream out her release, her body convulsing wildly against his hand. Brihanna didn't know up from down, her body still reeling. So when he mounted her, at long last sliding his thick cock inside her still contracting sheath—she screamed again.

After his first couple of strokes she tried to rise up, but his hand pushed her down.

"My god Brihanna, I'm trying to be gentle with you, but you feel so fucking good." Pressing against her back again he commanded, "Stay."

She stayed. Balling her fists into the sheets, only able to receive as he pressed into her over and over. Each stroke felt like he was stretching her to the limit. When he ran a finger down the middle of her back to her tailbone she gasped loudly. Somehow the simple act had set off sizzling vibrations in nerve endings she'd never felt before. When he went from measured strokes to a more thrusting tempo all she could do was thrash her head back and forth. Simultaneously wanting the torture to end, yet go on forever.

So when he ordered, "come for me baby" and smacked her ass, her body immediately obeyed. This time shattering around his dick, eliciting a loud groan from him. Then Brihanna was turned over, her leg muscles relieved to not be in the same position. Blinking back into coherency, she noticed the glistening condom he wore. Thank goodness! For once she'd been so out of her mind with lust she hadn't thought about protection. What was this man doing to her? Whatever it was he wasn't done, because his member was very much still large and alive.

Maneuvering her up the bed he kissed her stomach, murmuring praise. *"You're doing so well Baby Girl. You smell and feel so good!"* Then for the first time he touched her breasts, almost reverently. Gently squeezing and shaping them, before alternating suckling each nipple. Brihanna was still shaking, breathing hard as her body started to settle down. As it did, she reached out caressing his face, neck and shoulders.

It had just occurred to her that he was using this time to calm down too, when he paused and positioned a pillow under her head. Pulling her arms to either side of it before sitting up between her legs. He sat back, running his eyes over her, displayed as she was to him. When she saw unconstrained hunger in his eyes like he could feast on her for days, her heartbeat kicked up. Lawrence pushed her knees up, parting her thighs wider before sliding back inside.

As he pumped into her body, he candidly watched her. His hands roaming over her skin before settling on her breasts. Not surprisingly, he took his leisurely time as he played with them. Massaging her nipples to a firmer peak as he focused on them. This time firmly rubbing the delicate tips, squeezing and even twisting them. Stopping only to repeat it all over again from the beginning.

Somehow the pleasure became entwined, what he did above and below. A connection between her nipples and her privates formed, sensations from one, setting off the other. She was moaning, shaking, and having small spasms throughout her body as he worked her up the cliff of satisfaction once again.

"Come for me one *last* time." Lawrence's voice sounded strained to his own ears.

"I don't know if I can. It's too much!"

"Remember...you like taking my instruction, don't stop now."

Lawrence continued his slow stroking, then out of the blue sharply pinched a nipple. Her hands clenched around the pillow as an electric jolt traveled to her clit. A sound that was a strangled cry crawling up her throat.

"Mmmm Law, you're killing me!"

Lawrence felt his balls harden at the use of his nickname on her lips.

"You feel alive to me. But I can give you another *little death*. You *will* come for me Brihanna."

Leaning over her he began thrusting, hard and fast.

God yes! Did she think it or shout it? She wasn't sure as he was finally fucking her, grinding against her sensitive clit. If she died now, it would be a happy death. Then it happened, one spasm that flipped the switch and had her yelling out, snapping her legs against his hips. Letting go of the damn pillow to clutch at his back, her nails digging in as she broke apart. Lawrence's release followed, though she didn't know if he shouted out or not. She was deaf and blind to everything, except her own body's staggering response.

* * *

Steam from the shower fogged up the mirror as she adjusted her clothes in the bathroom. Brihanna's body still hummed with afterglow, how was that possible the morning after? Sleep was the only thing they'd done after that marathon session. She had been hoping for good and had gotten mind blowing. No lies told, her knees were still a little shaky. Combing her hair the best she could with her fingers, she shook off the strange thoughts and headed to the bedroom. But one glance at the empty bed and rumpled sheets had her immediately feeling a little aroused.

Snatching the purse Lawrence had brought in earlier along with her clothes, she turned quickly before the night's events played out in her head. Hightailing it to the living room to throw on her jacket, Brihanna put on her shoes then followed the sounds and smells to the kitchen. Where she found the man who had turned her body to putty, placing a second plate on the table. What did you say to someone who had obliterated your sexual world? He saved her from having to figure it out by speaking first.

"Good timing. I made us some breakfast...if you're hungry."

The man had no clue he was talking to someone whose idea of breakfast was heating up a biscuit sandwich in the oven so that it wasn't *as* gummy as the microwave version. The fluffy scrambled eggs, link sausage and waffles he'd made looked like a feast. Taking her phone out, she saw it was a little after ten-thirty.

"It looks great seriously, but I should probably be going."

Lawrence had been expecting this, so he sat down before responding.

"You sure? I know I'm pretty hungry after last night. Why don't you recharge before you run out."

If he hadn't brought up last night and added the word "run" she would have walked out the door. But now it was out there, like a silent challenge. Clenching her phone, Brihanna dropped in a seat.

"Fine, I could use some fuel. I have some errands to do that I'm already dreading, so I can't stay long."

Focused on eating, they fell into easy conversation, talking a little about the date along with a few topics from their chats. Both *were* starving, as they not only cleared their plate but a second helping in no time. Brihanna took a final swallow of her OJ before pushing back from the table.

"You want more sausage? Or I can whip you up another waffle, I love that waffle maker." Lawrence was pleased, as she rubbed her stomach in fullness.

"No, but I think I love your waffle maker too. Thanks for the food, it really hit the spot, but I gotta get home."

When he just nodded chewing the last bite on his fork, she stood up.

"Umm, do you want some help with the dishes or..." Brihanna threw out.

"No, I got it."

"Okay...well I'll see you." Brihanna turned her back. Suddenly, he wasn't very talkative, and she didn't appreciate how that made her feel awkward.

"Bri..." Lawrence said quietly.

"Yeah?" Stuffing her hands in her back pockets, she turned back.

"Thanks for taking me out for my birthday."

"You're welcome Lawrence, thanks for letting me."

"I *really* enjoyed my present as well. My question is did you?"

"I thought it was pretty obvious that I did. You're not fishing for compliments are you?"

"No," he shook his head slowly. "Just verifying, because I like us in *and* out of bed."

"Okay...your point?" She shifted her feet.

"I told you I wasn't looking for a one-night stand."

"I know, but you gave me what I needed and I gave you what you wanted. We're even."

"Are we keeping score?" Lawrence asked, setting his coffee down. "I think you're cool, I've enjoyed talking to you these past weeks and now hanging out with you. Knowing you can provide what I *need,* and handle what I *give* in the bedroom is a big plus to the equation."

Damn, but the man had a way with words.

"I'd be open," she glanced pointedly towards the hall, "to getting together again."

"Are you open to going on another date is what I'm more concerned with."

"Oh? You want to kinda kick it?"

"I want to do what we've basically been doing, which was talking and getting to know each other." Lawrence slowly smiled. "Then I want to add the going out and the sex, whenever you're in the mood."

"Like a try before you buy girlfriend?"

"I guess." Lawrence rubbed his chin, letting the phrase settle in his head. "But you know that goes both ways. I think they used to call it dating. I just know lately things either stay at a zero or go straight to a hundred between men and women. Folks either want to hook up with no connection or they want to leap into long term commitments after only being around someone a month. I think we connect, literally and figuratively."

Brihanna laughed a little nodding her head in agreement, before saying playfully. "I'm not sure I can take your application for potential boyfriend. I mean, I don't even know your credit score."

"It's 740 as of last week." Lawrence smiled briefly. "That's the type of information you need if you're looking to go half and half on a lease...which I'm not. I just want you to know this isn't a fly by night thing for me and I don't want it to be for you either."

Brihanna walked closer, and even though she felt butterflies in her stomach she leaned down and gave him a quick kiss before stepping back.

"Okay, we'll give it a try. Thanks again for breakfast." Brihanna winked. "And you know...for helping a sista out."

"Define *try* for me." Lawrence stood up, as she continued to back away.

"It means that I won't ignore your text or calls."

"Oh really?" He laughed still pursuing her as she reached the door. "I'm feeling special already."

"You should." Brihanna cheekily retorted, before hurrying out the house.

Lawrence let her go—for now. This was going to be interesting, one way or the other.

Chapter Seven

Brihanna had lied a little. The only errands she had to do were laundry and taking out the trash. Even though she was dog tired she loaded the machine before slapping a scarf on her head, loose pants on her legs and a snug t-shirt on her chest. Then she literally threw herself face down on the couch. She was exhausted! The trash would have to wait. Not wanting to fall asleep and smother herself, Brihanna slowly rolled over, a few muscles aching in protest, until she was looking at the ceiling.

What in the world had happened last night? And what in the hell had she agreed to with Lawrence? Groaning and covering her eyes she shook her head. How had wanting to get her rocks off, turned into "dating" the man. And this *man* was something she hadn't encountered before. He had "mood lighting" in his bedroom for god's sake!

He wasn't flashy, nor particularly loud. Yet, she could see him commanding a space with his quiet intensity. Probably part of the reason he'd become a manager at his age. He was cute for sure, but his appeal didn't come from his looks. He was a smart guy who could geek out, yet wasn't a geek. Often the other men in tech *she* ran into were at the extreme end of the geeky spectrum and that just didn't work for her.

Lawrence was the kind of guy that seemed to be at ease and fit in everywhere. She liked that about him. Being a black woman who *didn't* fit the wider narrative of what a black woman should be, dress, look, or act like, Brihanna appreciated a man who was secure in his own skin. She could only blame her upbringing for being turned off by weak, timid or unsure men. Whoever you were, just own that shit. Now, that wasn't to say she had no insecurities, doubts or frustrations but she liked who she was at the end of the day. While open to growing and shifting as life progressed, whoever she morphed into there was no doubt she would love that version too!

Speaking of...who the hell had been in that house getting turned on as a man commanded her about? Brihanna had never had a sexual encounter like that. She wasn't super experienced, only finding the courage *and* privacy to have sex when she was a high-school senior. College had found her open and willing for rendezvous, but she couldn't seem to meet many young men that held her attention long enough to earn bedroom privileges.

Add in being more interested in design and coding than dressing in the latest fashions and she'd ended up gaining less than a handful of lovers. Post-college the focus was getting into her field and becoming her version of an adult. Prying herself out from under her family's thumb as the youngest and becoming truly independent. In recent years most of her sexual interactions had been casual. A friend of a friend, a couple of hook-ups from on-line, that kind of thing. Two starts of a relationship that fizzled out were thrown in the mix.

Since she hadn't spent enough time with one man to feel comfortable doing some serious exploring in the bedroom, Brihanna accepted her sexual taste might not be well defined. *But* she would have bet money before last night that stripping in front of a man, and kneeling at his feet while she undressed him wasn't in her wheelhouse. The fact that doing both had aroused her was baffling. Her crazy ass had happily been submissive to his every demand. Had enjoyed the mix of roughness and softness of his touch *and* his words.

Yet, he never forced anything on her, he'd instructed and she'd taken his direction. *Too* eagerly and willingly to her mind was the problem. Parting her lips as even her conflicting thoughts had her breasts tingling. Her tender nipples had peaked just thinking of Lawrence. The hell with it! Fooling around with him could be exciting! Or it could all end horribly wrong. But the fact that it was the best sex of her life thus far, made it worth the risk.

Knowing if she kept thinking about last night she would end up molesting herself, Brihanna flung a hand out until it connected with her phone. Bringing it close, she started scrolling down the ignored texts from last night. Her ringer had been turned off since picking Lawrence up. Since the man had kept her thoroughly engaged all night, she hadn't even checked it.

Now Brihanna saw that everyone and their mama had contacted her! She had a voicemail from her mother, along with texts from Robert and Darrell. Even Tina, one of her two close female friends had wanted to hang out last night. Sending Tina a quick message apologizing for not hitting her back, she ignored the two from her immediate family. Replying to either might result in a call, especially from her mom. Sitting up she dialed Darrell back even as she secretly hoped he wouldn't pick up, but of course he did.

"Yo, what's up?"

"Nothing Dare, just getting around to your messages."

"Yeah, the next damn day." Darrell chuckled not annoyed in the least. "You must have gone out. Tell me it was with your cutie of a friend Danielle? You should stop blocking and let me hit that. She's always eyeballing me when I see her."

47

Brihanna cringed, even though she was used to his comments about her *other* close friend. "You are so damn crude. Dani doesn't want your ass."

"I know she doesn't...she wants this D I got."

"Keep your sick delusions to yourself. Besides, I wasn't with her or Tina."

"What did you get into then? Or were you just ignoring all humans?"

He knew his cousins sometimes needed a break, preferring machines or any make believe world not in this reality.

"No...I actually had a date."

Darrell let the silence stretch. Usually if she didn't want to talk about something she immediately changed the subject. Or continued right away if she wanted to share. He took the bait and nudged.

"Okay, go on."

Brihanna let out a pent-up breath. "It's nothing really. Just someone I met online a few weeks ago."

"Shit Bri, you didn't meet him at his house, did you? That shit can be-"

"This is the second time we've met actually. Each time in a public place." She omitted any answer about going to Lawrence's house or not. "We actually went skating."

"Okay then. That's cool."

Since Darrell's rare overprotective side had been appeased, she told him about their time at the rink. He was proud of her for winning at pool as he should be. He had been the main one to teach and practice with her.

"Sounds like a good time. What's this man's name and how old is he again?"

"Nice try. I never told you his age, and I'm not giving you his name yet either."

"Why the hell not? What is he trying to hide?"

"Nothing, I just don't want your nosy behind all in my business. Which in turn will pull Devon and Robert's nose into it, if not the entire clan. Besides, I'll tell you if we have a few more dates. I'm not sure if I'll be seeing him again."

Now she had told an outright lie.

"Whatever, we don't gossip like women."

Brihanna gave a truly amused laugh. "Yeah, keep fooling yourself with that thought."

"Seriously Bri, have you taken a pic of him and sent it to a friend, like we've told you to do?"

"Do you send your dates photos to one of *your* brothers when you hookup?"

"Get real Bri. Anyway, I don't do much online stuff anymore. Besides, I'm a man-"

"Oh, cut the crap."

Now her voice was tight. She was so sick of this gender crap they pulled on her. "You do know female killers have been on the rise the last two decades. Or that they often work with a male partner to jack and rob you. You're no safer than I am when meeting a stranger for some *strange*."

"Whoa, wait a minute. Calm down I'm just asking did you take basic precautions?"

Just as fast as she got mad, she got over it. Only because she could hear the genuine concern in his voice. She knew he was fussing out of love. Besides, he was her favorite cousin *and* her friend.

"Don't worry, someone in the family knows who he is if I go missing. Look I gotta go, I didn't get in until late last night. Much luv Cuz."

She used their way of saying "I love you" to let him know they were cool. While she understood where he was coming from it still irritated her. The men hadn't helped raise an idiot, so she hated when they failed to remember that.

"Much luv." Darrell sighed, knowing when he'd gotten on her nerves. "Later."

"Bye."

Hanging up just as her spin cycle stopped, she reluctantly went to put the clothes in the dryer. After that, she was taking a damn nap.

Chapter Eight

Lawrence didn't reach out to see if she got home after she left his house Sunday. He could just see her interpreting that as being clingy. So instead, he'd cleaned up the bedroom before falling asleep for a few hours. They didn't speak again until Monday when around three in the afternoon he got his first text from her.

Bri-Bri: You making it this Monday?
Lawrence: Yeah barely, still wishing it was 5 already though. You?
Bri-Bri: Dragging, someone wore me out☺
Lawrence: Ditto
Lawrence: I actually took a nap in my car at lunch. Needed to get away from annoying ass people too
Lawrence: BTW who calls you Bri-Bri?
Bri-Bri: No one if they know what's good for them
Lawrence: Got it, but it's cute like you
Bri-Bri: Whatever. Stay chill, later!

Lawrence let out a sigh of relief, then checked a few more things on his phone before putting it aside. He could admit he'd been nervous about coming on too strong, both during sex and after. He hadn't intended to expose her so completely to his brand of love making their first time. But the woman had been testing his control all night, turning him on with her smile, sassy wit and confident manner. Besides, it had been his birthday and he'd wanted to get down and dirty the way he preferred.

It had been too long since he'd had sex period, much less with a partner that seemed to thoroughly enjoy what he wanted to give. Thankfully, she seemed fine with how it all shook out. The fact that he would be seeing her again made his dick twitch under the desk. He immediately cut that thought off, pulling up the systems complaint queue instead.

He should probably remind himself just like he had her, that this was about more than sex. Part of why he was so good at problem solving was because he had a need to know how things worked. And Lawrence couldn't wait to find out what made Bri tick.

* * *

A couple of weeks went by and as the second week of June came it brought hotter weather that matched her dating life. They had gotten together for dinner the Wednesday after their night together, hitting up Jamaica's Fenton Jerk Chicken in Southfield. Brihanna had thought sex would change their dynamic. Thankfully it hadn't, well not where it mattered. They still had an easy rapport, the only change was an added simmering sexual awareness in the air. Which she didn't mind at all.

Upon dropping her off after dinner she asked him in. Lawrence had resisted, stating every date of theirs didn't have to end in sex. After rolling her eyes, she assured him that she knew her sexual rights. Informing him that she wanted another taste of him while she could. Pulling Lawrence inside, Brihanna hadn't waited for his mind to catch up. *She* sure as hell hadn't resisted when he demanded she sit on his face. Her panties that said "eat me" may have had something to do with that. Either way, she wasn't complaining when he made her come three times from it.

Good thing they got that session in, as by the time they hung out that Saturday, her womanly party pooper had arrived. But now her Aunt Flow was several days behind her and she was looking forward to getting some this weekend. Brihanna was outright giddy when she opened her door to him around eight.

"Hey cutie."

"You're not so bad yourself." She waved him in, at the same time snagging the bags from his hand. They contained the order of bibimbap and veggies egg rolls she had placed, along with some edamame to snack on later.

"Thanks for picking this up, how much do I owe you?"

"Not money." Lawrence declared, taking off his shoes before settling on the couch. "I know some other ways you can repay me Bri."

When she looked his way, he was suggestively licking his lips. A hot flash rippled over her body, as her mind went back to their last time together.

"Oh, so it's like that. Sex for food? I guess I'm okay with that since I can't cook for shit."

"Let me teach you some basic meals so you don't have to become a food-whore."

"I'm straight. I don't mind so much. As long as I get to choose who I'm bartering with."

He laughed, watching her pop a single edamame in her mouth before licking her fingers and wiggling her behind in delight. The sight made him shift in his seat.

"Brihanna, greet me."

"Huh?"

She glanced at him curiously though her mind was more on the food. But his face held the same intensity he wore during sex and she recognized the change in his voice when he spoke next.

"Greet me."

Heart already thumping a mile a minute, she let go of everything in her hands. "How?"

"It's not a complicated request. The way you would greet your man when you see him, with a kiss."

"Remember, you're my *maybe man*." She tried to inject some levity in the suddenly tense room.

He didn't chuckle, didn't lob a clever comment her way either, just repeated "Greet me, Brihanna." Using her government name in that way he had, that made her panties damp.

Closing the foot of space separating them, she put her mouth against his. This wasn't her first time taking the lead in a kiss, but it felt different from the others. Feathering kisses against his mouth she got little reaction. Pressing closer she used her thumb to stroke his jaw, then under his lips until he finally parted them, allowing her tongue to slip in. Slowly French kissing him, until she realized he was still barely responding. Giving a little tsk of frustration she pulled back.

"There, I did it."

"Hardly, do it again." When her eyes narrowed, he continued his instruction. "This time like you mean it. Like you're excited to see me. Like you can't wait to feel me between your legs again. You *do* want me deep inside you again...*right*?"

"Of course." Her answer was immediate, so fast that he cracked a brief smile.

"Then greet me again so that I can *feel* that need."

She hesitated, but then thought *the hell with it*. Grabbing him around the neck she slashed her mouth against his, hard and demanding. Forcing his soft lips to give. When they did, instead of backing off she got more aggressive, giving his tongue no choice but to duel with hers. Brihanna took it a step further, half climbing into his lap, tilting his head how *she* wanted, and stealing the air from them both. Letting out a loud moan of need that told the truth about how much she craved being in his arms again, skin to skin. Just the heated thoughts had her nails digging in his neck.

Lawrence was able to feel it alright, and boy did he respond, crushing her against him, giving as good as he got. When her hand went down and grabbed his manhood, he smiled against her lips before breaking away.

"That's how you say hello to your man Baby Girl. Every time it's just you and me, *that's* how you greet me, do you understand?"

"*Yesss* Law. Now let me say hello again."

Lawrence chuckled, but pushed her away.

"No, our food is getting cold. I was promised some TV if I played delivery man. You'll have plenty of time to pay me later."

*

Because of their busy schedules, the two decided to DVR the last season of *Game of Thrones* and watch it together. The show had ended last month and it had been hell not to read or have spoilers told to them. She figured they could watch three episodes tonight and another three tomorrow when they woke up. They were barely done eating when there was a knock at the door.

"Who the heck could that be?"

Popping the last bite of an eggroll in her mouth, she went to find out.

"You sure you didn't double-book your food deliveries?"

"Ha ha. At the moment you're my only food pimp."
Peeking out the peephole made Brihanna drop her head
against the door. "Shit, fuck."

On a sigh, she flung it open to address those on the
other side.

"I'm busy, which you know."

"And *that*...is why we're here."

"And that's why you need to leave." Brihanna snapped
an arm out to block the entrance.

The three women eyed each other. Damn her big
mouth. Of course she had eventually told her best friends
about Lawrence, the PG and rated R parts. She was keeping
the triple X stuff to herself. The mistake had been telling them
about the date tonight at her house. Now she had Tina and
Danielle squaring up in her doorway. They knew she wouldn't
back down without a fight.

"I got high." Danielle quickly called.

"Fine, I'll go low." Tina wasn't happy with the option,
but oh well.

"Hold up a minute ladies." Lawrence came to the door.
"I need Bri unharmed for the night...she owes me some
money. Come on in, let's see if we can work this out."

Chapter Nine

Her friends smirked, walking inside as Brihanna begrudgingly introduced everyone. Taking seats in the two spots opposite the couch, her friends immediately got nosy.

Wiggling her eyebrows Danielle asked, "So, what are you guys doing?"

"You know already because I told you yesterday. Catching up on GOT. Better question is what do you two want?"

Tina turned to Lawrence, shyly brushing her sisterlocs from her face.

"I'm sorry, she made me come. Bri has mentioned you a time or two and we wanted to meet you."

"Whatever, I didn't have to twist her arm." Danielle defended herself. "She's right about the rest. We felt like Bri was being stingy with details, so we wanted to come check you out."

Danielle's pretty, cinnamon complexion brightened with mischief, not embarrassment, as she reached her hand towards a box on the table. Only to have Brihanna slap it away.

"Hands, off. We just ate and don't have any leftovers for uninvited guests."

"Whatever, we just came from eating anyway."

Lawrence nudged Brihanna's shoulder. "I didn't know you were so stingy."

"Well, now you know." She pointed at the two women. "And now you two can go. You see he exists and hasn't killed me."

"Not yet." Lawrence whispered in her ear, before saying louder. "Why don't you two stay and watch with us?"

Brihanna fumed, "Danielle doesn't even like this show!"

"That's not true, I just don't understand it. I'm more into sci-fi than fantasy."

Tina, forever the peace maker between the two spoke up. "Thanks, we'd love to stay, *just* for a little while."

*

They settled down and returned to the show, but Brihanna was ticked off. She couldn't believe they would insert themselves like this. She snapped the edamame in her mouth like she wanted to snap their necks. This was overstepping big time! No warning, not a text or anything. The two hadn't even mentioned wanting to meet Lawrence when she talked about her plans. Anyway, who cared what they wanted! If she decided to never introduce them then that was her choice.

Lawrence didn't seem to mind as they peppered him with questions, and Danielle bugged everyone trying to understand the show. Every time Brihanna made eye contact with one of the women her temper sored. When they were about ten minutes into the second episode, she couldn't stand it anymore. Going into the kitchen on a pretext before she lost it, and poor Lawrence thought she was a crazy woman. Staring at nothing while she tried to calm down, Brihanna jumped when Lawrence squeezed her from behind.

"Are you okay?"

"No, I'm not okay." The words rushed out of her mouth in an angry whisper. "I'm pissed and two seconds from throwing them out, *after* telling them about themselves."

"Come on, why are you so upset? It's not like they interrupted us getting it on."

"I would have completely ignored the door in that case, but that's not the point."

"Then help me understand?" Lawrence was puzzled on why this was a big deal. "We were going to watch TV anyway. Only difference now is two more people in the room."

"Keyword *we*. I wanted to watch this show with *you*. Someone who loves the show as much as I do. Not a person who doesn't understand it and another who is a casual fan."

"Okay, I can appreciate that, but your friends seem cool! I don't mind getting to know them and vice versa."

When Brihanna thinned her lips only to glare at him, he scratched his head. "Unless you have a problem with me doing that."

"Don't even go there! I clearly talk about you so you're no hidden secret. And what the fuck if you were? My business is just that, mine. They were disrespectful coming over here when no one asked them to. If I wanted them to meet you then *I* would have asked them *and* you. Then set it up in a way that worked for everyone. Not in the middle of someone else's plans!"

Well damn, she was really mad about this. Reaching for her shoulder, Brihanna batted him away. *Okay...*

"If it helps, I don't think they meant any harm, just curious and maybe wanted to look out for you."

"Don't take up for them. They're being nosy, rude and inconsiderate."

"I just don't think it's anything to get upset about."

"Look, let's say one weekend you told me you and your boys were going to chill at your house and I say *sure no problem.* Then that night I show up out the blue talking about *I just want to meet them and hang out.* We're not talking about when someone's says they're going to sit at home doing nothing and you surprise them with drinks or tickets to a concert or something. But when people *know* you had plans with other *people* but they decide to insert themselves anyway. Would you like that?"

Lawrence thought about it before slowly shaking his head.

"You got me. I wouldn't like that at all, I'm sorry. Look, I invited them in, I can tell them to go. Then we can finish out the night the way we planned. Some killing onscreen and bedroom payments later."

"I don't need you to fight my battles." Brihanna said testily.

"I'm not. I'm just trying to fix what I messed up." Lawrence breathed out his nose, now *he* was getting a little annoyed. "I don't mind telling them to scram."

"No. My friends, my problem. They disrespected *me.* I'll handle it. And I'm not in the mood anymore tonight, so you can feel free to leave with them if that makes a difference."

Shit on a stick! How had this spiraled out of control where she was about to show him the door?

"It doesn't make a difference, I'm still staying overnight. Sex is a perk for us both. If you're kicking them out let's get it over with, so we can salvage our non-sex night and at *least* enjoy the rest of the show."

"Fine."

Marching back over to the sitting area, she bit her cheek so she didn't yell, "*Get the hell out!*" Instead, she went with something a tad less brisk.

"It's been real. You don't gotta go home, but you gotta get the hell up outta here." Okay, so that wasn't much different, but whatever.

"But the second epis…" When Tina saw Bri's face she trailed off, grabbing her purse off the floor and standing. "Um, yeah. I guess it's about time we go. Come on Dani."

Danielle stood too. "You could at least let us finish this one."

"Look, you lucky you got in the door. You came, you saw, you chilled. Now get your rude, watch-party crashing asses out my house."

"Okay, we're going." Danielle hustled out the angry woman's reach.

Brihanna stalked them to the door until they stood on the other side.

"I'm sorry, Bri. We didn't mean to ruin your night or get you upset." Tina offered the apology while Danielle just rolled her eyes.

"Thanks, I'll get over it…but not tonight."

"I think you're tripping. I don't see the big-"

Brihanna slammed the door in Danielle's face.

"You feel better now?" Lawrence asked.

"Actually, I do." Turning around grinning, she asked, "Do you mind if we restart this one?"

"We can do anything you want. I'm trying to stay on your good side for the rest of the night."

"I'm surprised I lasted that long, it runs in the family. My brother and I are slow to anger, but when we do, watch out."

"Is the same true for your cousins?"

"Ehh, kind of. For my older two yes. For the younger ones Dare and Dev, they have flash tempers. Doesn't take much to get them going amongst the family at least."

"Hmm," Putting his arm around her shoulders, Lawrence pulled her in tight. "I'll have to remember that."

*

They finished watching half the episodes like they planned, and by the time they called it a night things had been back to normal. Except the playful sexual vibe the night had started with. After showering and breakfast, they settled in to finish the show. By the time it was over in the early afternoon, they knew why folks had signed petitions asking for a final season redo. They debated and half argued over the various outcomes of the show.

"I can't believe you were okay with that part!" She hit him with a pillow.

"We'll agree to disagree. I personally thought that made sense all things considered."

"Whatever."

Falling into comfortable silence as Lawrence switched sites and flipped through Netflix, Brihanna took the time to study him. She was impressed overall on how he'd handled the entire situation last night. Even though she personally wouldn't have let those heifers in, he hadn't become irritated at their arrival. Deftly dealing with her flare of temper as well, she had to give him extra points for not making up some excuse to leave once getting some was off the table.

Even with spending more time together they still had a lot to learn about each other. It had been only a month since they met, barely enough time to scratch the surface. Taking the thrilling sex out of the calculation, she liked his personality, not to mention all the interests they shared. Add back *in* the sex, and she might have a bonafide winner on her hands. She was lightly smirking when Lawrence interrupted her thoughts with a question.

"Hey, I forgot to ask last night but do you want to go to Comic-Con next month?"

"What...did you say?"

"Do you want to go to Comic-Con, you know the one at Cobo."

"I thought that's what I heard but couldn't *believe* it. Hell yeah, I want to go!"

Launching herself in his lap she started kissing all over his face.

"I'm not complaining." Lawrence stated chuckling. "But I wasn't expecting this reaction."

"You don't understand. I've only been twice, both times by myself. I can't even *pay* friends or family to go with me."

"Really? I try to go at least every other year. Figured it was something you might like."

"I'm so excited! *Ooohh*, can we dress up too? I don't care what we each go as, just something."

Lawrence shrugged. "Sure, why not."

"Thank you, thank you, *thank you!*" Brihanna said still raining kisses.

Climbing completely in his lap, she glued her mouth to his. When she pulled back, she ran her tongue across his bottom lip. "I am *so* ready to make that payment now."

"Best believe I'm eager and ready to take it."

* * *

Four days later Brihanna found herself on her Aunt Dolores' doorstep. While both her mom and aunt lived in Southfield too, they actually respected her privacy. Never doing random pop ups, in fact they rarely stopped by at all. She was the one usually visiting them, like she was now as she waited for her aunt to pick up the phone.

"Hey Aunt D! Are you busy? Do you mind if I drop by for a minute?"

"Hi yourself, it's been awhile. Yeah, come on by, I'm home."

"Good, come open the door. I'm outside."

Brihanna laughed as her aunt fussed and told her off, not hanging up the phone as she walked to the door.

"Girl, get on in here. Why'd you even bother to call knowing you were outside?"

"Look, I don't assume anything. You could have had company."

Dolores fluffed her hair and winked. "You're right on that point, one never knows."

"Plus, I knew you were here." Brihanna continued. "You didn't put your car in the garage. You know if the boys see that they'll fuss at you."

They sat down at the kitchen table and Dolores waved that comment away.

"I don't pay my fussing boys any mind."

"They have a point Aunt D. It's not smart to put your car up at night instead of when you first get home."

"What night?" She threw her hands up, looking around. "It's not even six-thirty in the evening on a summer day. Did they forget I spent most of my life in Detroit and never had issues? I know how to handle myself!"

As her aunt continued to go off, Brihanna let her mind drift. It was true, both her mother and aunt had grown up and then raised their families in the city, and neither had any problems that the kids knew of. Still they were getting older, it was time to leave unnecessary risks behind. Brihanna wisely kept that opinion to herself, again she wasn't stupid. Drumming her fingers against the table, she finally stopped the tirade.

"You done?"

Dolores narrowed her eyes and thought about popping her nieces hand. "Yeah, I'm done. What did you come over here for anyway?"

"I wanted to talk to you about something. Get your opinion."

"Shoot, you know that's one thing I love to give and you don't even have to ask me for it."

"Don't I know it." Brihanna mumbled. "Anyway, you have to promise not to mention this to Mama. *Any* of it."

Dolores sat up with interest, leaning across the table.

"Is it something your mother needs to know?"

"I'm serious Aunt D."

"I am too. Is it?"

Brihanna's face looked as if a sour lemon had been popped in her mouth. "Absolutely not."

"Okay, then she won't know it from me. Brihanna you're a grown woman, I respect your right to decide what you share and *not* share with your mother."

"Thanks."

Deep down Brihanna knew that, which was why she'd come here in the first place. She had been wanting to talk to someone about this for a while, and after last weekend she knew her friends *were not* a good choice. *Yes,* she was still mad at them and she bet they couldn't stand her right now either. The nature of her issue prevented her from talking it out with her cousins or brother. Her mother wasn't an option. As much as she called herself an independent, modern, "I don't care what you think" person—she cringed thinking about bringing this up with her mom.

"Girl, spit it out. I could be taking my nap, or my evening drink."

"Sorry, this is a bit delicate. So, don't freak out but I've been dating someone recently."

Brihanna expected theatrics, maybe a "hallelujah" for good measure. Instead, her aunt's eyes got big, blinking once before she nodded her head.

"Got it, go on Brihanna."

"We've had sex."

One of Aunt D's eyebrows went up.

"It's *really* great sex."

Now, the other rose. "Girl, I'm not seeing an issue so far, hell it sounds good to me!"

"I...well he..."

Brihanna trailed off getting flustered. Swiping hair from her face, she decided to do it like removing a Band-Aid, quick and fast.

"He likes to be controlling in the bedroom." She rushed the statement out.

"Controlling how?" Dolores frowned confused, "Is he doing anything you don't like or hurting you?"

"No!" The question surprised a small laugh from Brihanna. Why would she stick around for that? "It's nothing like that, remember I said the sex was great."

"Brihanna, sometimes you work my nerves. Get to the damn issue."

"I was trying to. He's demanding, aggressive in a controlled way. We do things that I'm not used to. I don't know, I guess I'm wondering if it's normal to like stuff like that. Before this, I *never* would have thought I'd be doing some of the things we do. It feels a bit kinky."

"*Ahh.*" Dolores sat back in her chair smirking. "There's nothing wrong with you. You've found a lover that makes a different side of you come out. It's like trying new food that doesn't look good. You think you'll hate it and you end up loving it. Then it becomes one of your favorites."

"That actually makes sense. I just didn't think of myself as having a kinky side."

"Ha! Every woman does, it just takes the right man to bring out the freak. As long as you're good with everything that's being done *and* that you're doing. There's nothing wrong with *whatever* two adults do together. Different strokes for different folks."

"You think so?"

Thinking of this as some kind of sexual awakening, a rite of passage made Brihanna feel better about the fact she *loved* everything they did.

"What we do, gets a little out there." Brihanna tried to infer, without actually explaining.

"Does it now?" Dolores interest was roused. "All I can say, is if it feels natural and good to *you,* then don't be ashamed of it. Sexuality is expressed differently for everybody. I for one, am glad it's not all one flavor. Why don't you give me an example, just so I can make sure it's all on the up and up."

"I don't think so." Laughing, feeling much lighter Brihanna got up. "But I thank you for the advice, I feel better now."

"Come on, we're both women! What you think ya'll the first generation that has tried some freaky shit in the bedroom? Like your grandma said rest her soul, there is nothing new under the sun. Why, I can tell you when *and* in what position your mother conceived both you *and* your brother!"

"Aunt Dolores!"

"You want to know yours? Might explain why you like, what you like. Your mother was standing up doing-"

"Nope, nope. I refuse to hear this."

"I get it. You're still young and shy. It's because you didn't have a sister to talk smut with while growing up. Just tell me, stop being so stingy. Share the excitement."

Dolores slid a pen and notepad across the table.

"Come on, draw me a picture and let me guess. It'll be like charades."

"You are sick!" Brihanna snorted with laughter. "But I love you anyway! Thanks again."

"Yeah, yeah, you're welcome. It runs in the family, now you know where you got it from. Get on out of here. Be safe, whatever the hell you doing. Remember, we don't do babies in this family unless a husband is attached to them."

Chapter Ten

Michigan Comic-Con arrived mid-July and Brihanna had never been so excited. They were going Saturday so she wouldn't have to rush getting ready Friday after work. Plus, she wanted to enjoy this experience to the fullest. Michigan held several Comic Conventions in the summer, this one was in the Cobo Center downtown.

The weekend event was filled with comic books, toys, video games, anime, cosplay, artwork, and apparel. Not to mention the Star Wars and Star Trek stuff, in addition to industry professionals and celebrities that would be in attendance. Brihanna didn't care what Lawrence dressed up as, it just had to be a real character. He refused to tell her who he'd picked. Conversely she'd been just as secretive, wanting that shock value when he saw her.

Eagerness had her getting over being mad at her friends quicker than she planned. Tina wanting to get back in her good graces was more than happy to help. And Brihanna hadn't hesitated, roping the woman into helping her find things she needed for an outfit. Now the day had arrived! Brihanna was stuffing her ID in her phone carrying case which doubled as a wallet, waiting for Lawrence to arrive. He had barely knocked when she flung the door wide. One glance at his outfit and she was all over him giving him a kiss of greeting he wouldn't soon forget.

"*Well*, hello to you too."

"I put a little extra in there because of your outfit. I can't believe we match!"

"I can't tell since you have on that trench coat looking like Inspector Gadget."

"Shut up, I figured we wouldn't make it out the house if I gave you a kiss in my costume."

Once she took it off, Lawrence totally agreed with her. He had to swallow a couple of times before he could find his voice.

"Wow."

"You like? I made it my own by adding this and that."

She was dressed as Nubia, the black sister of Wonder Woman. Starting with an easy to find Wonder Woman outfit of red, blue and gold, she then modified it to fit her needs. In some comics, the warrior had gold plates down the middle of her torso. Brihanna had taken some gold foil and a glue gun to create the effect, opting for silver gauntlets on her wrist, medium size gold stars for earrings, topped off by a bold red lipstick.

"Oh wait! Let me get my headpiece."

She leaned over the sofa snatching up a gold banded tiara. As a nod to the original creation, she had glued a big fake red jewel to its middle, representing a red feather. Deciding to have fun with her hair, she'd used one of those rub in dyes that were all the rage. First making her hair a jet black, then putting streaks of electric blue in them. Another nod to the older comics where the characters hair was blue-black. Tina added some clip-on extensions to make the hair fall to her shoulder blades.

"*Sooo*, what do you think?" Brihanna asked twirling around in her completed outfit.

"I think...you made the right decision with the coat. You look sexy as hell! I feel like you're trying to give me a heart attack."

"You can take it." Smirking, she patted him on the chest. "After all, you're Superman. That's why we match, our outfits have the same colors at least."

"*You* look great. You don't think I half-assed it do you?" Lawrence asked.

"No, I get it. It's like you were caught changing into Superman."

He had on dress pants over the traditional costume, so that his bottom half was Clark Kent while the top was Superman, cape and all.

"Good, I just couldn't bring myself to walk around in public with my junk displayed in spandex all day."

"It's probably for the best, you'd be distracting most of the women and some of the men. Can't have that, it's a family friendly event. Are you ready? Because I'm *so* ready!" Brihanna squirmed with excitement.

"Yeah, let's roll. Wait, why do you have on a name tag?"

A fancy, slim tag that read NUBIA was on her upper chest.

"Because I don't want anyone to get confused, I'm Nubia, the black champion made at the same time as Diana. Matter of fact...hold on."

She went running to her kitchen to come back thirty seconds later, slapping a gold tag on his chest. It simply read Earth-23.

"There you go, just so they know."

"The canon black Superman." He couldn't help but give her a quick peck for knowing that. "Thanks Baby Girl, now let's get out of here."

One Click For Love

* * *

Arriving around one they found parking was already crazy. Which surprised no one for a gorgeous summer day in downtown Detroit. The Comic convention was just one of many events happening over the weekend. They started getting attention as they traveled down the long halls to the main exhibit entrance. When she caught the first person taking a picture, she conscripted them to take one for her as well. Selfies were cool but not when you were trying to get a full body shot.

The pair jumped right in, getting their conference guidebook and started making the rounds. Right around then Brihanna grabbed his hand and started towing him along, rarely letting it go the rest of the day. If Lawrence was being honest, he was still in awe of how good she looked. He had never minded much being branded a nerd while growing up. The term and status had been making a positive comeback in his day, not enough to make him cool, but enough so he hadn't been a pariah either.

So yeah, in high school and beyond he'd looked at his fair share of animated porn so to speak. Sexy visuals of female characters from games, books and shows. But seeing her joyfully dressed as she was, was different. *She* was sexy, confident and comfortable. That last one may have seemed like an odd positive to include but it was the one that turned him on the most.

In his experience, it was hard to find a women who embraced every part of themselves. A woman who didn't shy away from all the nooks and crannies of their personality. It was probably why they were so compatible in the bedroom. Other women often couldn't seem to let go, too afraid of being vulnerable.

Brihanna seemed to have no problem with his heavy hand during sex. Even better, minutes after sexing she was still confident and commanding as ever. She was just as comfortable showing him her submissive side, as she was with her pissed off one. Never apologetic or embarrassed about either. And now he was getting a look at yet another facet. The kid like joy of dressing up as your favorite superhero radiated out of her eyes. Her entire demeanor screamed, "I'm the shit and I dare anyone to say otherwise!"

People didn't realize there were all kinds of ways to dictate to others. He enjoyed her brashness and got a thrill out of her boldness. Like those panties she wore that silently told a man what she needed, wanted and craved. Damn his train of thought! Nothing good could come of him thinking about those scraps of materials *speaking* to him, at least not while he was in this crowd. So, he was relieved when they finally made it to their first guest speaker, Phil LaMarr, a famous black voice and screen actor.

Phil was known best for his role on MadTV, though they both knew him better as the voice of Samurai Jack and the black Green Lantern in the Justice League cartoons. Not to mention, he voiced Conrad for the offbeat Futurama they were both fond of. The guy had been doing acting and voiceover for more than twenty years. The two were keenly listening as he spoke about his career and took questions. After, they managed to get a picture with him before they were moved along with the tide of the crowd.

Navigating to a few tables and started buying souvenirs. His date was thrilled by it all, and frankly, so was he. He was feeling downright ecstatic to share the types of things he liked fully with a lady by his side who enjoyed it to. Next Brihanna wanted to check out a video game voiceover actor. Charlet Chung who was in a popular game called Overwatch, he'd actually played it a time or two.

Not surprisingly Charlet was just as excited to meet Brihanna, someone who brought the characters she voiced to life. The two chatted and Bri even gave her a business card. Then of course both women wanted a picture on their phones, before he jumped in for a group one. He didn't want to miss being in the middle of two beautiful women. He was a Blerd not an idiot.

As four p.m. hit they were starving, taking a break to grab some food. By five, they were checking out one of the independent films being spotlighted. When that let out they spent the next few hours circling around the venue checking out things they had missed. Until they were back at a small Lego display that was set up in the area Dan Veesenmeyer had spoken.

He was a Lego illustrator who had worked on Lego Star Wars and on the upcoming Lego Marvels Avengers video game. Because of Brihanna's work they had sat in on his presentation earlier, but had to rush off to the next thing before viewing the Lego scenes. The detail you could put into those little blocks was amazing. He'd always been astonished that a plastic child's toy could make a unique art of its own. Lawrence read an article a while back that spoke of a Lego Master Builder who sold his creations, sometimes for over six figures. When they finally wandered away from that, he saw Brihanna check her phone.

"Everything good?"

"Yeah, just checking the time. It's after 7:30, is there anything else you want to see that we didn't hit?"

"No, you?"

"Nope." Grinning hugely, she tilted her head giving him a soft lingering kiss. "I'm good. I had a terrific time. Thank you so much for today."

"My pleasure. I should be thanking *you*. This is the best Comic-Con I've ever been to. You want to stop somewhere for dinner?"

"No. There's enough at my place to throw something together. I'm ready to get out these heels!"

They were walking towards the exit when they were stopped for the 10th time by someone asking to take a selfie. More than one person had thought they were paid models for the convention. Not to mention the other dozen who had snapped pictures from across the room like the first guy Brihanna caught. This guy, and not the first of the night, wanted a picture with just Brihanna. Lawrence obliged then handed back his phone.

"Thanks! I just had to get a pic. Your outfit is awesome! One question, since you're Nubia why are you wearing the lasso? That's a Wonder Woman only weapon."

"Why? Because I wanted to. Let's just say I took it from sister dear, and she didn't object...much."

The evil yet happy grin Brihanna leveled at the man was priceless. There was decades of "who gon check me boo?" wrapped up in that look. Lawrence loved it! Slinging an arm around her shoulder they left laughing.

* * *

Brihanna still felt jittery, like she was hopped up on candy as they walked in her building.

"I loved today, but I'm glad to be home."

"Who you telling, I feel grimy after walking around in this suit all day."

"You know, I think I've seen folks with just the upper half of the outfit before." Brihanna was carefully taking off her tiara.

"Yeah, I found that out *after* I decided I didn't want to wear the entire thing." Lawrence regretfully reflected. "I thought about ordering it, but it wouldn't arrive in time."

"I'll help you out of your tight onesie, if you help me out of these boots and we can share a shower."

"Deal."

Brihanna wore a shower cap, wanting to make sure her color didn't wash out, she planned to rock her hair next week at work. In-between a little play time with Lawrence, she showered before escaping to dry off. When he stepped out about five minutes later, she was in the bedroom drying her feet. He looked yummy slinking in with a towel wrapped low on his waist.

"That hit the spot."

"Funny you said that." Brihanna picked up the lasso next to her, eyes twinkling with friskiness. "I was thinking maybe I should give you a few whacks. Think you would like it?"

"Not sure, maybe." He came closer, grabbing the end. "But, I know what I *would* like."

"What's that?" Brihanna probed softly.

Lawrence caressed several inches of the fake rope. "I'd love to tie you up with this."

Chapter Eleven

"I'm game."

Giving her a look of hesitation, Lawrence sat next to her.

"Brihanna, I was just playing. You don't have to-"

"I don't need you to tell me that, I'm aware. I meant what *I* said. I wouldn't mind trying some rope play."

"Well damn." He was shocked but also delighted. "The treats just keep coming today."

Brihanna nodded, loosening his towel.

"That's how I feel too. I figured why not try something new to cap it off...if that's okay with you?"

"Hell yes! I mean sure, whatever."

As he tried to hide his eagerness, Brihanna giggled, because with that rising penis of his it wasn't working. Walking her fingers up his chest before kissing his jaw, she brought up another subject.

"But before we do, I've been thinking, we should have a safe word."

Okay, something else out of her tantalizing red mouth he hadn't been expecting.

"Can't say anyone has ever needed one. I'm good at realizing when a woman has had enough. You don't feel like you can't tell me no, or to stop do you?"

"Didn't we just talk about this?" Brihanna asked confused. "No, I don't have any problem telling you anything."

"Good, I'll never do anything you're truly uncomfortable with." Lawrence needed to be sure she understood that. "It's about pushing boundaries a little, relinquishing a little control. That's all."

It was important that *this* woman understood where he was coming from.

"I know all of that." Giving him another soft kiss, she went on. "Stop being weird. Let me tell you the word I picked out!"

"You've really thought about this?" Lawrence laughed amazed at the unflappable, spirited woman in his arms. He was a lucky man, and if she wanted to play so did he.

"It's been a thought on my mind. Okay what about *terminate*?"

"I think." Lawrence started playing with her nipples, lightly running his thumbs across them. "That's a long word for you to try to get out."

He was probably right. She already felt tongue tied and he was barely doing anything.

"You have a point." Brihanna pouted prettily, fondling his cock. "You suggest something then."

"Hmmm, what about *endgame*? That's connected to comics *and* video games."

"I actually like that." Liked that one of his hands was between her legs too. "But I feel like it's too soon, with the movie and all, it's depressing."

"It's going to be depressing for *me,* when you want to stop."

"You'll get over it." Brihanna grinned, caressing his balls. "Let's go with *abort*. It's short, direct and to the point."

"Abort it is Baby Girl. Now hand me that rope. You have the perfect headboard for what we're about to do.

*

Brihanna kept possession of the coveted rope, long enough for her to queue up "When We" by Tank on her phone, and place it on her dresser.

"I put it on repeat."

"That's what you want to hear the whole time?" Lawrence was intrigued.

"Why not? Seems appropriate."

Lifting an eyebrow at that response, he just moved his hand in a "gimme" motion. Brihanna took her time walking over, handing over the rope just as the words, *recipe for disaster*" filled the room. She was feeling cheeky and totally uninhibited tonight.

"Get right in the middle of the bed." Lawrence gave her a light slap on the ass to move her along.

The song and his commands giving her a jolt of energy down to her toes. As she laid there waiting while he suited up, her mind started to swirl with erratic thoughts. Like the fact her headboard *was* perfect, though she hadn't bought the open rail design for the purpose of being tied up. When he leaned over looping the prop around the post, she licked at his skin, which smelled of her body wash of cucumber and green tea. Running her hands over his back, Brihanna used what little time she had left to grope his flesh. From his rounded ass to his chest, anywhere she could reach.

"Naughty, naughty Bri. You know you're going to pay."

Her actions were adding to the anticipation already rushing through his blood. Thank goodness she couldn't see his hands shaking.

"Oh, I *know*." She scraped her teeth across his nipple. "It will be worth it. I like touching you, and the way you feel."

He rose up and caught her devilish hands, dragging them above her head.

"Didn't anyone ever teach you to keep your hands to yourself? You've been driving me crazy all day. If I didn't love looking at your delectable bare body, I would have kept you in the outfit."

"Maybe next time."

The ravenous look in his eyes and the feel of rope touching her wrist, made her squirm. When he moved his focus to looping her hands together, she cleared her throat.

"Have you done this before?"

"Yes, once. Stop talking Brihanna, unless it's to scream out my name."

She didn't speak again but nipped his forearm in rebellion. Finished, Lawrence slid down her body, letting his weight press her down. Taking her misbehaving mouth he sucked at her tongue hard. Shoving his daylong pent up need, into the plundering kiss. When she was totally breathless he finally lifted up, ready to enjoy the gift beneath him.

He took his time, building a slow burn by raining bites, licks and caresses down her body. Finally reaching her thighs before trailing his tongue over her clit and through her folds. But he didn't stop there, instead parting her thighs while pushing her knees up. Bending down he put his teeth around the fleshy part of a toned thigh. Then he slowly increased the pressure, before turning his head to the other side. Marking as *his*, what would be cradling him later in the night.

Lawrence left a wet trail up to the back of her knee. Lips worshipped along her muscled calves, until finally he was massaging her foot. Once he'd paid the same attention to the other leg, he turned back to the jewel between her thighs. Dipping inside, his tongue found her wet and ready.

"My baby girl is always extra wet for me. That makes me feel special. I think I should reward you for that."

Lawrence got comfortable, putting his lips to her swollen clit. Thrilling at the sound of gratification that echoed around the room. He placed her legs around his shoulders before sliding two fingers in her slick, hot canal. Then he went to work—with his tongue, lips, fingers and even his teeth to drive her wild.

Brihanna fucked his face—with the scant leverage her hips and legs provided. Marked thighs pressing against his head in enthusiasm only egged him on. She came twice and when she was on the verge of coming a third time he suddenly pulled back. Face wet with her juices, he took her legs and pushed them towards her head, effectively making her immobile. Not hesitating before sliding into her tightness. *Oh, so slowly* until he couldn't go any further.

"*Law!*"

Brihanna screamed, breaking around his thickness. The orgasm more intense as she strained against him and the rope. He didn't let her come down from it either, starting to move, making the ripples start all over again. Deep stroking slowly, he was big, long and hard and each pump filled her to capacity. He was leaned over her body, and every stroke had him brushing her exposed clit. Brihanna couldn't stop coming!

It was too much, the pressure, the pleasure all rolled into one.

"*I can't, I just can't...abort*"

"Do you *really* mean it?" Lawrence purred in her ear. "You really want me to stop?"

Time stood still, but when he withdrew she instantly felt deprived.

"*Damn you Law. No I don't!*" She got out shakily.

Lawrence went back to work. "Told you. I know what you *need.*"

Stroke.

"What you can *take.*"

Stroke.

"What you can *give.*"

And then he switched it up on her, giving her two quick shallow thrusts, followed by a deep one. He was driving her mad! Had her scratching and pulling against her restraints. A moment before Brihanna reached that invisible limit, he was gone. Lowering her jittery legs, putting his face back between her thighs, only to make her whimper anew. This was a sweet kind of torture, but torture nevertheless.

Lawrence gave one last lick upwards then rolled her pliable body. Pulling her up unto her knees he entered her from behind. His pace was quicker now, less constrained. He was getting close to his own finish line, yet struggling to keep it at bay. She felt *so fucking good*. Nothing in life should feel this remarkable. He wasn't even sure he deserved this much pleasure, which was why he always tried to give it back to her in spades.

Brihanna was thrusting back to meet him, even as she held on to the metal headboard as it smacked into the wall. That she continued to trust him, wanting him as much as he wanted her, was monumental. Reaching forward he pulled the slipknot, releasing her hands.

"This is crazy! Law, I think I'm about to come again."

"No you're not." he pulled her up so they were both sitting on their knees, his front pressed to her back. Slowing his strokes. "Not yet."

Brihanna groaned deep and long. How did he expect her to survive this, while he teased her nipples?

"I need to come *now*."

"No you don't." They were both sweaty, panting and struggling to hold on. "Not until I tell you to."

He crossed one arm over her chest, his hand cupping the base of her neck. His other snaking down to her core, tickling the bud of nerves with his fingers.

"Ooohh, no fair! I can't hold out."

"You *can* and you will." He firmed the hand at her throat. "Do it for me Baby Girl."

It was like his words had power. Somehow, she persevered as a tidal wave of bliss bloomed in her core once again. But this time it felt like it was all over her body, even her scalp was tingling.

"*Please!*" She begged.

He could feel the pulse in her neck drumming like crazy, matching the pounding of his heart. Circling and pressing down hard on her nub, he gave them both permission to let go.

"Come for us Bri."

Brihanna let the ecstasy wash over and consume her body, then flow into Lawrence. After that she couldn't think, couldn't reason and could barely breathe.

And it was fan-fucking-tastic!

Chapter Twelve

Brihanna shuffled back to bed, completely tired from the long day and utterly drained from the mind-bending sex. Snuggling against him under the thin summer sheet, she applied a tiny pinch to wake him up.

"Leave me alone, you're not the only one worn out."

"Superman doesn't get tired. Besides, I want to ask you something."

"He does after dealing with Nubia." That earned him a harder poke with a sharp nail. "Ask Bri."

"Why do you enjoy being extra dominant? You know...during sex."

That woke his ass up. Had Lawrence sitting up against the very headboard she'd just been tied to.

"I want to give you the bullshit answer of 'I don't know' but I won't. I analyze most things including myself. I came to the best conclusion I can figure out years ago. Are you sure you want to hear it? Like a lot of things that shape people it barely makes sense."

"That's okay, I still want to know."

Nudging herself under his arm, she hugged his waist. Wanting him to know he wouldn't be alone when he shared a piece of himself.

"Whatever it is, had a part in shaping you. I *like* who you are, so nothing you say will change that."

"Hmmm, okay." Lawrence wasn't so sure. "My mom and dad had some issues. A good relationship that went

84

downhill when I was close to turning nine. He got fired from his plant job but was lucky enough to get something else pretty quick. But it was less money, harder work. A little time went by and he started drinking more. You know how the rest goes...in short order he was a true alcoholic.

He wasn't a happy drunk either. Picking fights inside and outside the home. It escalated to him hitting my mom every few months. By the time I was ten, I started jumping in to protect her and started getting it too. Which only made the fights between them worse. Fast forward another year and someone on the streets took care of our problem for us.

Guess he picked a fight his fists couldn't win. Someone stabbed him over a petty argument he most likely started. I wish I could say I was happy, but it hurt when he died. Bri, I didn't hate him. Most of my memories of him were as a good father. He shared my love of comics and movies. I remember him taking me to Vault of Midnight, a comic store shortly after it opened in the city. I was seven and I was excited by the books, but more by having a special day with just the two of us. Plus, he told me to pick out seven books to match my age. Said it would be the start of my collection. We did that every year around my birthday...up until he died."

"I'm so sorry. That's horrible you lost a good father to a bad situation. Is that why..."

Lawrence rubbed a hand down her back, shaking his head.

"Yes and no. It's why I don't drink often or heavily. Liquor makes you lose control. I guess that put a seed in my head that keeping control was important. But it was an incident five years later when I was sixteen that I believe cemented that need for me. And that eventually made its way into my sex life."

"What happened?" Brihanna glanced up at him, even though he was still looking straight ahead.

"Being slightly nerdy was never a big issue for me. Overall, I grew up surrounded by people who believed in hard work and education in my family, neighborhood *and* school. That didn't mean there weren't some people who started shit with me every once in a while. Walking home one day I left my cousins behind, macking on some girls. I figured I'd be waiting on them forever as they tried to get some play.

I was a good block, block and a half ahead of them, pretty close to their house when some dudes from school started to talk shit. Normally, I ignored stuff like this and kept it moving. I did the same that day too, until one said, 'yeah, keep walking before I put you in the dirt like someone did your weak ass daddy'.

Til this day I don't know if it was their laughter or the fact that the anniversary of his death was the week before, but I snapped. Dropped all my shit and just swung on him. At the time I didn't know if the other two were trying to get me off or jump me, but I beat their asses too, until they ran away. It was like a red haze came over me.

Learned later one was running home, passed my cousins on the way and told them I was crazy. That I was killing Tony, the guy who mouthed off. I remember my cousins screaming my name, trying to pull me off. I lashed out at them too, which is when Mike ran home to get help and Malcolm stayed behind still trying to stop me. It took my uncle putting me in a chokehold and dragging me off before I started to think again and calm down. My uncle had already called an ambulance. Told my cousins to take me to the house and for all of us to stay there no matter what."

"Jesus, Lawrence! What happened to Tony? Please tell me he didn't die."

Lawrence mouth hardened and he could feel his heart beating fast like he was there again. It had been years since he'd thought about any of this in detail.

"Thank God, he didn't. My uncle risked going to jail and losing his family to stay until the ambulance and police arrived. They believed the lie he told of not knowing who did it. That he was just a good Samaritan. We were all surprised they didn't jump to conclusions."

"He must love you very much."

"Uncle Luc? Yeah, he does, but he also felt guilty." Lawrence pinched his eyes shut before blinking. "See, he's my mom's big brother. Felt bad he hadn't known what was going on with her and me in the bad years. He told me later he wasn't going to fail to protect me again. Or let his sister's only child go to prison if he could help it."

"But didn't Tony or one of the other boys tell the police it was you?" Brihanna wondered aloud. "Other people had to have seen it?"

"The entire thing probably lasted five or six minutes max. School had let out awhile back and most parents were still at work. Because my cousins had been taking all day most of the other kids who lived close by were home already, not that many witnesses."

"But the ones you beat down?"

"Bri, they were scared shitless of me after that. I went full berserker on them, *and* my cousins. Those guys were all too afraid, along with anyone else who saw it. I never got any shit after that day from *anybody*."

"Damn...and Tony, how bad was he hurt."

"Bad enough, he had broken ribs, a broken nose and a very bad concussion. He was in a coma for a full day and had bruising in other places. Had to stay in the hospital for five days, but he made a full recovery. No lasting damage, but he *could* have died. I almost killed someone all because I lost my temper."

The pain and disgust she heard in his voice, hurt her heart.

"I'm so sorry *any* of that happened."

"So am I. I couldn't believe I'd been even worse than my old man. That I had that kind of violence in me. I *never* wanted to be like him, a drunk, someone who liked to use his fists. It's why I took pains to stay out of drama. I think after the fight I over compensated. Tried to order and control as much as possible in my life. Like I said weird...but there it is."

When she backed away he glanced at her for a few seconds, not able to hold her eyes long. Brihanna wasn't having it, grabbing his chin so he had no choice but to face her.

"Had you ever been in a fight before that?"

"No, if you don't count my dad."

"Were you ever in a fight *after* that, for any reason?"

"No."

"That's because it's not you, it's not who you are." Letting his chin go to stroke his face she pointed out gently. "Don't you see that? Why did you feel like you were some big risk?"

"Because my father was never a hothead either. From everything folks told me and that I remember, he was a cool, affable guy that people liked being around. Until one day he wasn't."

"Lawrence, that's because of the alcohol and from what you told me maybe some depression at the start. Alcohol can make some folks turn into entirely different people."

"Does it? Or does it just allow people to be who they really are?"

Brihanna tried another tactic. "Did your mother and uncle think you were some violent time bomb just waiting to go off?"

"No, they didn't actually." Even now he sounded mystified by this fact. "My mom was very disappointed and scared that I'd go to jail. She made me get a job and for the next year I had to give 80% of whatever I made to a fund set up to help Tony's parents pay hospital bills. I was a good kid, got great grades that we both planned I'd use to get me in college. She was terrified I'd derailed my future, but she was never afraid *of* me."

"Exactly. And your uncle what did he think of you after that day?"

"He actually thought it was bound to happen. Not what I did to Tony, but that I'd have an outburst one day. He felt I never grieved properly over my father and maybe he was right. It was hard to grieve for someone you'd been afraid of for the last two odd years. Someone who hurt you and the mother you loved. Yet, someone you loved *in spite* of that. Hell, I didn't know what to feel or how to act when he was gone. Uncle Luc was always telling my mother that I was *too* much of a good kid, that I never let go and just acted like a bad ass teen. He said he'd seen for years I was holding myself "to tight" and that one day I'd snap."

"Sounds like a smart man. And your cousins, did they disown you or stop hanging with you?"

"Of course not!" Lawrence looked like the prospect was bizarre. "We're still tight to this day. You know that. They went out of their way to stay on my good side for a while, but other than that they treated me like normal."

"That's the point I'm trying to make. That those who knew you best, knew *that* one moment wasn't you. I appreciate you sharing all this with me. I didn't mean to open up old wounds."

"Hey, you had no clue it would be a downer. I want you to feel comfortable to ask me questions."

It was depressing but also freeing to speak about this with someone else. No other woman had ever asked or wanted to look beneath the surface of the actions. To discover the "why" that made him who he was.

"Tell me more about your family. You mention your brother and that one cousin *a lot*."

"Yeah, I do."

Brihanna understood he needed for a distraction. Past hurts had a way of still feeling fresh despite time.

"I think I mentioned I grew up as a tomboy. I've always had one or two female friends at school, but my home life was filled with my brother and our four cousins. We're all really close, basically grew up on top of each other."

Brihanna laughed a little, swiping her long tresses out of her face. Closing her eyes, she talked about the most important men in her life.

"All of us had our own version of daddy issues. For me and my brother, it was abandonment. My mom's husband, our father, just up and left shortly after I was born. Too much for him to handle or some shit. Anyway, my brother has been my hero since I could talk. He's been taking care of me since he was barely out of diapers, *literally*.

Then I became his shadow. I look up to Robert the most, but my cousins aren't far behind. Thomas and Edward are the oldest and we got to learn from their mistakes. They spent a lot of time trying to corral the rest of us. My younger two cousins, Devon and Darrell are the wilder ones of the crew. My brother fell somewhere in the middle of being a hell-raiser and caretaker. I considered Dare, I mean Darrell my best friend while growing up. We're the closest in age and any time I felt I couldn't go to the others I turned to him. Let's just say my family is a unique bunch.

Don't get me wrong they're all good men, the best in fact. But can also be arrogant, stubborn and prideful to a fault sometimes. On the flip side you get very smart, protective men who can be a lot of fun. They raised me, so blame them for any bad habits and traits. I can't forget my Mom and Aunt, they shaped the boys who then shaped me. Two examples of hard working, loving women who also had a wide streak of 'taking no nonsense' in them.

Being the baby and the only girl, added a different level of scrutiny and meddlesomeness from the entire clan. There were a few times it felt suffocating growing up. But I always knew I was loved, knew each of them had my back. And that made me feel invincible when life had its moments...you know."

"They sound formidable."

Yawning she nodded, "They are, and crazy too."

When Brihanna tried to hide a second yawn against his chest, he slid down so they could lay flat.

"Explains why you were able to pull off your costume so well."

"I did rock it, didn't I. Thanks again for sharing with me Law." Brihanna was exhausted, physically and mentally.

"I should be thanking *you*."

"For what?" She barely got out, already falling asleep.

"For everything." Lawrence tenderly whispered, kissing the top of her Nubia colored head.

"Go to sleep, Baby Girl. I'll be watching over you now."

Chapter Thirteen

Brihanna was about to do something she'd *never* planned on doing. That's why she was calling her sister-in-law, fully prepared to whine if need be. This fact didn't make her proud, but she didn't want to do this alone. She was pacing her bedroom waiting for Mika to answer.

"Hey little Sis, what's up?"

"Hi. I have a favor to ask." Brihanna said rushing the sentence out.

"Hmm, do you now?" This got Mika's attention and she put down her Monday after work drink. "Go on."

"Are you busy tomorrow night?"

"Maybe," Mika hedged. "Depends on what you say next."

"I need you to go somewhere with me, I'd prefer not to go by myself."

"Okay, I'll go." And just like that Mika was in.

"But you can't tell Robert or *anyone* else what we're doing."

"Hell, why didn't you say that up front. Now I'm really in! I love a good secret. What are we doing exactly?"

"Just meet me at my place tomorrow at six, you'll be home before nine."

"Ooohh, I hope it's something good!"

"Well...it's *something*." Brihanna responded warily. "Anyway, thanks and don't be late."

"I won't. Gotta go, your brother's coming!"

* * *

Mika wasn't late, in fact her sis-in-law showed up at her condo at 5:40.

"I told you don't be late, *not* to be early." Brihanna grumbled, opening the door and waving her inside.

"I didn't know how traffic would be, so I left work exactly on time. Give me a break and give me a glass of water. It's hot!"

Brihanna agreed, it was hot as heck this mid-August. Handing her a cold bottle of H2O, watching as she chugged it down.

"You know," Mika pointed out. "Your place could use a tad more color. Or a picture or two on the walls that isn't inspired by a video game."

"You said that the last time you were here. I told you these three scenes are from the first games I programmed."

"I remember and I didn't say get rid of them. I said *add* to the wall." Changing the subject Mika asked, "Tell me we're getting some food before we do whatever. Also, tell me what the heck we're doing?"

"No, finish that water. We might as well leave early since you're here. Though I suggest you use the bathroom before we go."

"Why? Are we going somewhere that doesn't have them?" Mika grinned until she saw Brihanna wasn't joking. "Where *exactly* are we going?"

*

Soon enough Mika found out their final destination, but now she was more confused than ever. Brihanna had acted like a crackhead, all jumpy and nervous on the ride over. Leaving the car and walking to the Schoolcraft College entrance, she couldn't hold her questions anymore.

"Umm, are you going to night school or something? And if so why do you need me?"

Scowling, Brihanna led her down a hallway, stopping in front of a classroom.

"Look, just be cool and do this thing with me...at least for tonight."

"Okay fine." Mika threw her hands up. "One night, no more questions asked. But I'm really hoping it's a painting class that includes naked men."

Brihanna shook her head opening the door, where they were welcomed by a woman who looked twenty if she was a day. They were quickly handed a black apron and hairnet. The woman marked their names from a list, then pointed towards a back workstation.

Mika put on the apron before wrestling with the hideous net, which would only fit the front area of her big hair. Turning to her blushing in-law, Mika slowly slid her finger across her throat in the younger woman's direction. But she didn't have time to say anything as a person passing out instructions came by.

The class was starting.

This was the third one and they were about to bake and frost a small two-layer cake. Once the instructor who thankfully looked old enough to teach went over some basics, they were left to their own devices. Brihanna and Mika followed the others to the sinks to wash their hands, then on to the pantry gathering ingredients on the list. On their way back Mika hip checked her, nearly sending her into the doorframe! Gritting her teeth Brihanna let it go. Figuring she deserved it for dragging her to what was a nightmare to them both.

Back at the *Master Chef* set up of a station, they got started combining ingredients. They were baking what should be a simple two-layer vanilla and lemon cake. While everyone else chattered easily with their partners, she and Mika were concentrating on the recipe like it would be on a test the next day. Two young apprentices walked around the room just in case anyone needed help. They somehow ended up with cake batter in pans and were opening their ovens around the same time as everyone else.

The cakes would take between 25 to 30 minutes and the instructor encouraged everyone to do a quick cleanup. Ten minutes later they got new instructions for making homemade icing. It seemed easy enough with only four things to mix together. But when Mika found out she could add not only different flavors but coloring too, she had a field day mixing up four different bowls. Mika could have her rainbow cake, Brihanna had stuck with the recipe. She would be happy with a result that *looked* edible.

The pair were extremely relieved when their cakes came out more or less normal. Brihanna's were a little flat but not too bad, while Mika's were sunken a bit in the middle. Getting them out of the pans without losing much of their cake bottoms was a struggle. They were told to take another clean up break if needed, which would double as time for the cakes to cool before moving on to decorating. When it was all said and done, they both had a two-layer cake, one with a mildly yellow frosting and the other looking like an explosion of Fruity Pebbles.

"I can't believe you're documenting this." Brihanna snickered, watching Mika take a picture of her creation.

"I can't believe you're not." Mika snapped a photo before the other woman could hide her face. "There, I did it for you."

"Delete that right now!" They had just started covertly tussling over the phone when the instructor spoke.

"Good job class! Looks like everyone more or less has a cake! Now as always, the real test is in how it tastes. As you used the same batter for each layer it doesn't matter how you cut it. Get a slice and take a bite! We'll be coming around as well."

They decided to be each other's taste testers and as they swapped forks, their expressions were comical. It turned out Mika had used way too much sugar in both her cake *and* icings, while Brihanna had somehow added salt to her batter. A *lot* of it. The teacher came around, wanting to check on the new class members himself. They tried to dissuade him from eating anything, but he insisted. He should have listened. The man ended up walking away with his mouth twisted and halfheartedly telling them they'd do better on Thursday. While everyone else was wrapping their dessert to take home, they both dumped theirs in the trash before heading out.

* * *

"Please, bring us waters quickly! I'll also have a margarita." Mika begged the man who sat them down at the Chili's a block up the street.

The waiter grinned, then turned. "And for you? Anything to drink besides the water?"

"No, thank you." Brihanna was driving after all.

After drinking almost all their water, which didn't fully erase the horrible taste from their mouths, they looked at the menus. It was after eight-thirty and neither had eaten yet.

"Are you going to tell me *why* you made us take a cooking class where we almost poisoned ourselves? Or do I have to beat it out of you. I kinda *want* to beat it out of you, so feel free to be stubborn."

"You'd try. And you might succeed since your cake is causing me to go into a diabetic coma."

Mika didn't respond as she was taking a big gulp of the alcoholic drink just handed to her. They quickly put in their order before turning back to the conversation.

"I have taste buds again. Now tell me, or that picture is going online."

"I just wanted to try something different." Brihanna sighed, playing with the fork on the table. "Thought it made sense to be able to cook a half decent meal for myself...or others."

Clucking her tongue Mika nodded, then asked softly, "So...who is he?"

The surprised widening of eyes gave Brihanna away, even as she denied it.

"Why can't I want to learn to cook for myself? I'm getting older and I think my metabolism is funny acting. I wanted to make a change, so what?"

"I totally agree...so what if you want to make a change for a man, it's no big deal." Mika kept right on talking as Brihanna got fired up. "So how long do these classes go for?"

"Twice a week through the end of October. Twenty-two classes left."

"I see, that's a lot. Bet they cost a pretty penny too."

"Yeah, they sure aren't cheap. Schoolcraft has a good culinary school reputation." As Mika grimaced Brihanna rushed on. "But I planned to pay for us both...*if* you want to finish the class with me."

"Free cooking classes...let me think on it."

Brihanna dropped the subject and they shared the entrees brought out. She watched the outspoken woman send a text and figured it was to Robert checking in. The two ended up poking fun at each other's cooking, cracking up about the disasters their cakes turned out to be. For dessert they split a molten chocolate cake and Mika returned to the topic of the classes.

"If you tell me who he is, I'll take the classes with you."

"There is no he. I'm doing this for my-"

"It's cool if you want to take the classes by yourself. After tonight I can understand why you wouldn't want anyone else to taste your cooking."

Brihanna snapped her mouth shut, crossing her arms in annoyance. After staring each other down for ten seconds Brihanna gave up.

"Ugh, fine! But I'm not doing it *just* for him and I don't care if you believe me. You remember that site where you updated my profile awhile back?"

"Yeah."

"And that date I went on, I've been dating him since then."

"I knew it!" Mika bounced in her seat. "I mean I didn't know it was him, but I knew you were dating someone! You don't come by as much anymore, don't answer your texts as quickly on the weekends either."

"Lower your voice Nancy Drew, you got me. And how do you know about my text response speed? You almost never text me."

"Because I have to hear Robert complain about it. It must be a sibling thing because he worries about you more than he should. Anyway, I can't believe you're dating the cutie I picked out for you!"

"I won't argue about who picked him. But yes, we're seeing each other."

"Aww, I think that's awesome. Someone's caught Brihanna's eye!" Mika said the last in a sing-song voice.

"Don't get sappy about it."

"Umm hmm."

Was all Mika said, turning her head deep in thought? Eventually she turned back, giving Brihanna a wistful smile.

"You know, I think it's cute that "part" of the reason you want these lessons is because of him. There is nothing wrong with that. Cooking, for family or a romantic partner has always been a way to show you care for them, appreciate them, another way to tend to them. I agree it shouldn't be an obligation or a required skill for a woman, that's some old-fashioned shit. But I think it can be a sweet and intimate thing to do. That's the *only* reason I'll take the classes with you. I wouldn't mind showing an arrogant someone I know, appreciation in a different manner."

"Oh my God, thank you!"

Brihanna was elated and relieved she wouldn't be struggling alone. She didn't know why the idea of getting this wrong bugged her so much. If she had to put the blame somewhere it would be on her mother and aunt for harassing her about this lack of skill for *years*.

"I figure when we finish we can rub it in everyone's face."

"Agreed." Mika snorted. "You must really like this guy. When do I meet the man who broke you off *so damn good,* it made you want to cook? You know you'll have to introduce him to your brother right?"

"Whoa!" Brihanna looked appalled. She couldn't even wrap her mind around putting Lawrence through the gauntlet that was her brother.

"I didn't say I liked him *that* much!"

Chapter Fourteen

How had she allowed Mika to talk her into this dinner with her brother and Lawrence? The cooking classes had been rocky at first, then gotten better as classes continued. Brihanna still hadn't told anyone else about it, not her friends or family. She almost told Darrell one day knowing he would keep it a secret, but there was one problem. He would have teased her mercilessly in private and she didn't have time for that. So it stayed her and Mika's secret, well mostly.

Mika had to tell Robert who she was spending time with. Otherwise, he would have gone off his rocker thinking she was having some weekly affair. However, he had no clue *what* they were doing. Robert tried to coax it from her one evening when she dropped by, but Brihanna promptly told him to mind his business. Besides, she was pretty sure Robert thought it was some scheme his wife had cooked up, and she wasn't going to tell him any different.

Mika was handling telling Robert about his sister's "friend" and the dinner in general, which meant Brihanna had to deal with Lawrence. By unspoken agreement the pair tended to alternate their time at each other's places. So the Saturday before this proposed dinner, they were laid up together on her couch when she brought up the get together.

"Law, can I ask you something?"

"Anything Baby Girl."

Brihanna had to pause a moment, still not quite used to the ease in which they were now using their bedroom pet names in regular conversation. It wasn't that she didn't like it, it was just very intimate, this out in the open expression of what began as private affection. But it made her feel connected to him on a nonsexual level.

"Did you forget what you were about to say?" Lawrence probed.

"Sorry, I got distracted. I wanted to know if you had plans next Saturday?"

"Pretty sure I'm clear. I assumed I'd be spending it with you."

"Yeah, so about that. I was hoping you wouldn't mind going to dinner at my brother's house. His wife invited us. I told her I'd have to ask you though…"

Lawrence sat up, taking her with him, his mind analyzing what this meant. He knew already how central of a role her brother played in her life. He'd be meeting the de facto head of her family, no doubt about it. And no matter how people tried to slice it, that usually implied a deep relationship between two people.

It was one thing to meet her friends, which some women even took *that* as a sign of "official togetherness". It wasn't that he didn't consider them in a relationship, because he did. But meeting her brother would be defining it as "a serious one". Was he ready for that?

"Hey," Brihanna pinched his side. "Cat got your tongue or what?"

"Just thinking. It'll be just your brother and wife, right?"

"Yep, just those two."

Lawrence ran his thumb across her bottom lip so she wouldn't bite it. A habit she had when nervous or uncertain.

"Do *you* want me to go?"

It was a real question, because he could see in her eyes she *almost* hoped he would say no.

"I've had a couple of days to think about it and honestly yes, I do. But *only* if you truly feel comfortable going. We can get together with them at a later date. It doesn't have to be now."

He was silent, thinking on it some more. When he broke it down it was really simple. He had no intentions of not seeing Brihanna for the foreseeable future, which meant that it was inevitable that their relationship was headed for a firmer status sooner than later anyway. Therefore, one week or one month didn't really make a difference.

"I'd be happy to meet your brother. Just let me know the details and I'll add it to my schedule."

"Okay." She said quietly, a little shocked he'd agreed to the madness, then louder to confirm. "Okay then, I'll text them to you."

"Cool." Lawrence broke into a real smile. "Any tips on how to handle him?"

"Not really, he's a crafty one so you never know what to expect. Honestly, I don't know which of the two you should be more worried about, him or Mika."

"Sounds like I'll just have to be on my best game."

Brihanna buried her face against his chest, laughing in apprehension. "This is going to be a hot mess."

* * *

The second day of November was sunny but borderline cold, as one would expect for the month. As two thirty rolled near it was time for Mika to do her part in all this. She headed to the basement, breaching Robert's man-cave.

"Hey, what are you doing?"

"Nothing." Robert glanced over. "What's up?"

"Don't you have anything to do today?"

Sighing, he sat up from half lounging on the sectional.

"Why? Do you want to go out or something?"

"Nope." She sat next to him. "I'm surprised *you* don't. Don't you want to go down to the gym, or go visit Cam or your cousins for a few hours?"

"Not really. I was happy relaxing before my bothersome wife came to bug me."

"Why don't you go out and enjoy the nice day!"

"It's below 60. I'm good right here." Robert looked at her like she was crazier than normal, then back at the screen.

After a few seconds pretending to watch television Mika tried again.

"Well, do you mind running some errands for me?"

"What's wrong with your legs?"

"I just want to catch up on some housework is all. I can make a list if you-"

"Naw, uh-uh." Challengingly, he leaned forward until they were almost nose to nose. "Why are you trying to get me out of the house?"

"I'm not-"

"Mika..."

Hearing his "I'm losing patience" tone, she decided to go for a close version of the truth.

"You got me! I'm planning a surprise for you and need you out the house for a few hours."

Robert bit his tongue, stopping his first thought from coming out. He'd learned that it paid not to be as blunt as his first mind. He considered himself a very smart man, though even an idiot would know acting ungrateful when your wife was doing something nice, was asking for trouble. Even if you were *just* trying to fucking relax. Marriage was a humbling experience for Robert.

"Shit Mika...for how long?"

"Until about six. Actually, if you could make sure you're back by 5:45 that would be *perfect*."

"What in the world...fine, whatever. I'll go entertain myself somewhere else."

"Thank you, Baby!" Mika gave him a smack of a kiss, before hopping up. "And don't be late!"

Robert watched her excellent ass jog up the steps before he rose. Did her surprising him mean he had to do something back?

"Shit."

These damn marriage parameters were going to be the death of him.

*

When they heard the front door open at exactly 5:45, Mika wiped her hands on a rag, before whipping off her apron.

"You stay in the kitchen and let me handle this."

"I don't know why you're nervous. I'm the one whose boy...whose friend, is about to get grilled."

"Probably because I haven't told your brother about Lawrence yet."

"What!"

"Hush, just stay in here." Mika warned before rushing out.

Mika *was* nervous, and not just because she was literally ambushing Robert with their guest of honor. No, she was nervous about her cooking too. The one other time she had cooked him something besides breakfast, was when they'd returned from their honeymoon. It had been a disaster. Though considering how bad it was tonight could only be an improvement.

"Hey! You're on time."

"I'm always on time." Robert replied dryly, looking his wife over.

She had changed clothes into a semi-dressy outfit and even had a little makeup on. He'd gone over it in his head while sitting in a sports bar, and he was sure he hadn't forgotten any special dates. Yet, here she was dressed like they were celebrating something. Plus, he could smell enticing scents coming from the kitchen. She must have wanted him out of the house while a catering company delivered dinner. Hell, knowing Mika a hired chef might be in the house.

"You look nice, and whatever we're having smells great."

"I'm glad you think so!" Mika smiled brilliantly, wrapping her arms around his waist. "Because we're having a special dinner."

"I put two and two together. What's the occasion?"

"I figured now would be a good time for you to meet Brihanna's boyfriend. The one she's been dating for over five months."

"Wait a minute." Robert stepped back indignant. "She mentioned months ago she was casually dating someone. Now it's a boyfriend?"

"*Its* name is Lawrence. Maybe I misspoke, maybe it's still casual. You can ask the man yourself when he arrives."

"The hell you can." Brihanna stepped into sight from her eavesdropping spot. "I don't want you grilling him. All I want is to have a nice casual, low-key dinner so you can meet."

"Everybody stop saying casual." Robert snapped out. "When it's clear there's nothing *casual* about this."

He raked his eyes over his sister. She too had on light makeup, and a long-sleeve swing-dress that hit her knee-high boots. While not particularly fancy it was a *dress*, something his sister *very* rarely wore unless it was mandatory.

"Casual my ass. You're both dressed up and if this wasn't such a big deal you wouldn't have sprung it on me last minute."

"Sorry," Mika waved her hand. "That's on me. I figured it would be better if you didn't have time to overthink it like you're doing now. And we're not that extra dressed up. Though if you want you have a few mins to go throw on something-"

"I'm not changing for someone I didn't even know was coming, to *my house!*"

Oh boy. Both women looked at each other knowing Robert was inching towards "pissed". Mika tried deescalating his temper.

"Of course not, it doesn't matter what you wear. This is a sit down between family and *friends.*"

"Just when is this...Lawrence arriving?"

"Six." Brihanna sighed. "Look, I'm asking you as a favor to just be normal and give him a chance."

Robert looked at his watch, it was 5:54. "I make no promises since I've been blindsided."

When both women were silent, Robert ran an agitated hand over his head. Any other time they'd be going toe to toe with him. His sister must really like this guy, if she pulled Mika in to double team him.

"Both of you can stop the pouting. I know how to be civilized."

"I don't pout but thank you!" Brihanna gave him a quick hug, just as the doorbell rang.

"Ooohh look, you already have something in common with him." Mika gushed. "He's exactly five minutes early, as to be on time, but not too early to be an inconvenience. My mother would love him."

"I'll let him in." Brihanna tried to move past Robert but he blocked her path.

"I don't think so. I'll be the one getting the door."

Chapter Fifteen

Robert opened the door, to see a man slightly shorter than him standing outside. Dressed in navy dress pants and a blue and white plaid button down shirt, hair cut low and trimmed, though Robert did notice a design cut low in the back. Before either could speak, Brihanna ignoring his instructions tried to walk past him again.

Robert slung a possessive arm around his sister's shoulder, tugging her to his side. That only put an amused smile on the man's face, which Robert watched turn into another type of smile all together. The man took in his sister from head to toe and lingered *too* damn long on her booted legs.

Conclusion—Robert didn't like him.

"Hey." He said gruffly which didn't seem to deter the man, who sent him an easy smile before stepping inside extending a hand.

"I'm Lawrence Townsend, nice to meet you."

As they shook Robert didn't speak, but Brihanna took the opportunity to leave his side.

"Lawrence, this is my brother Robert and my sister-in-law Mika."

Mika threaded an arm through her husband's and held on tight. "What a pleasure to meet you. I've heard a lot of good things about you!"

"*I* haven't heard shi-" Robert bit off his words as Mika squeezed him. Disengaging from her grip, he shut the door.

"Come on in, apparently we're having dinner."

They sat across from the "couple" as the food was passed around. Robert wasn't surprised that Mika kept the conversation going, while he remained mostly silent, watching and listening. He found out that Lawrence wasn't a big drinker when he insisted on water for dinner, saying maybe he'd have a drink later. He could only shake his head upon learning that his wife had a hand in how the two met. It was quickly obvious the pair shared a lot in common and enjoyed the same things, so he could see why they got along. Everything he was hearing added up.

But he wanted to know what was *keeping* his sister interested? Brihanna was by no means shy, but as a whole had never been a true people person. She could be playful and an outright pain in the ass with family and those she got to know. But it took her a while to warm up, something they had in common as siblings. Where they got it from he wasn't sure, as their mother was sweet and outgoing. Quick to have a kind word for anyone she ran into. Perhaps it was their abandonment issues. Another thing he'd like to punch their father for if he wasn't already dead.

So, it was understandable that the first adult *man*, that Brihanna went through all *this* trouble to introduce to him, got his hackles up. Who was this man who looked at his sister with heavy lidded eyes when he thought no one was looking? What made him special? Once Brihanna got over her irritation with him and what he suspected was a little nervousness, Robert saw her relax. Falling into the normal banter she had with Mika. Robert noted Lawrence had no problem flowing into an easy rhythm with both women.

The man across from him seemed laid back and confident. Not bothered by the deadpan look continuously leveled at him, or Robert's near silence. He gave the man props for remaining cool *and* for keeping his hands to himself while at the table. Thank goodness they weren't lovey-dovey, though Lawrence *had* very briefly massaged Brihanna's neck earlier. Yeah, he'd seen that, he'd seen it all. Regretfully, he hadn't heard or seen anything that would justify him warning the man off his sister, *yet.*

"Everything was really good." Robert finally volunteered an original comment, as Mika brought in a pretty, little two-layer cake. "What company did you get this catered from?"

The question had the two women looking at each other before Brihanna turned to Lawrence.

"What do you think? Did you like everything?"

"Yeah, that's why my plate is clean, I wasn't trying to be polite. Everything was great. That pasta salad was spot on! If the place does take-out let me know. I'd get some of that once a week."

Brihanna started to grin, while Mika outright laughed and passed around the last plate of cake.

"What's so funny?" Robert didn't get the joke.

"Well, remember I said this was a special dinner." Mika sat down. "I didn't just mean because Lawrence was gracing us with his cute face. Me and Brihanna cooked. And no, *we* don't do take out."

There was silence for about three seconds before Lawrence's amusement filled the room.

"Bri...*you* made this?"

"Hey!" Brihanna punched him lightly on the shoulder, though she was grinning from ear to ear. "You don't have to laugh so hard."

Mika wished she had her camera ready, the look of shock on her husband's face was incomparable.

Slowly putting down his forkful of cake, Robert's dark brown skin took on an ashy look, while his eyes darted between the women.

"But...neither of you know how to cook. Brihanna you burn toast!"

"Why are you telling all my business? Besides, that's mostly because I lose track of time."

Ignoring her excuse, Robert turned to his wife still flabbergasted.

"*You* don't have the patience to follow a simple recipe much less something complicated."

"You might be right," Mika's face got tight. "But you're still an ass for saying so. Brihanna and I took cooking classes. Yes, we sucked before but we're intelligent women, so we *learned*. Is that so hard to believe?"

Comprehension dawned on Roberts face, but even so he still shook his head.

"So that's what you were doing twice a week. I still can't believe it. I need a real drink!"

Robert rose and walked out the room. Brihanna had a boyfriend *and* two women with a pen cap worth of cooking skills between them, produced a delicious dinner. He was feeling like he was in an episode of The Outer Limits.

While the other man was gone, Lawrence hooked an arm around Brihanna's neck, pulling her close.

"Good job, Baby Girl!" He gave her a kiss on the forehead. "I'm impressed."

"Thanks! I just wanted to try something new, no big deal."

"Don't be dismissive, learning a new skill is always a good thing." Then Lawrence whispered in her ear. "I'm going to miss being your food pimp though."

So that she didn't make a fool of herself over his praise, she pushed his cake closer.

"Well, you haven't eaten this yet. Can't be a success if it sucks."

Robert walked back in with two glasses of scotch, to a glaring Mika who was shoving cake in her mouth.

"See the next time I cook for you." Mika's feelings were hurt. "You don't even appreciate it."

Robert sat, sliding the second glass across the table to Lawrence before addressing the landmine he'd stepped on with his wife.

"I'm sorry Princess, I do appreciate it. I'm just in shock. Everything was excellent, I mean it. Let me eat this cake, I'm sure it's just as good."

Reaching for his plate, Robert was too slow as Mika snatched it out his grasp before standing up.

"No cake for you." Reaching over the table she snatched Lawrence's plate too. "Or you. The only people who deserve cake are me and Brihanna. You two go away."

"Well, damn." On a heavy sigh, Robert rose and nodded to the other man. "Come on, I think we've been dismissed. Let me show you around."

* * *

Robert led the way down the steps slowly, still trying to shake the disconcerting thought of his wife cooking, not to mention the hole he had to dig himself out of later. Right now he needed a clear head to deal with this guy dating his sister.

"This is where I go when I get in trouble to avoid the wife." Waving a hand to indicate the space. "You ever been married?"

"Cool area. I'm a bit of a gamer myself and have my basement decked out for it." Lawrence was taking his time slowly walking around. Looking at the sports memorabilia along the walls and shelves.

"Also no, to your question. Bri tells me it'll be your first anniversary before the month is out."

"Yeah, that's right. What else did she tell you?"

Robert had let him wander around, but now came to stand near him. At his question, the man met his eyes and for the first time Robert saw a flash of annoyance in them.

"The regular things a person talks about when they're dating. She's told me about her family and talks about you the most."

By his tone, Robert didn't think Lawrence liked that fact much. Well, *too damn bad*. Chuckling a little, Robert was ready to have some fun.

"Funny, she never told me about you. I just learned your name tonight. She mentioned going out a couple times with someone a few months ago...but it didn't sound like it was anything special."

Lawrence shook off his irritation. There was no way he was going to fall for what the man was trying to do, which was to put him on the defensive.

"That doesn't surprise me. She's mentioned you can be...overprotective even though she's a fully-grown woman. I've met and hung out with her friends months ago. When we first started seeing each other it was semi-casual."

Lawrence took a step closer, and the next words that came out of his mouth sounded like a challenge.

"However, things change and I'm standing here in front of you. You can say... things progressed."

"Did they now?" Robert raised an eyebrow not intimidated in the least. "How exactly have they progressed?"

"That would be Brihanna's and my business. I'm sure she'll let you know, *if* she thinks you should."

Robert laughed in earnest now. Looked like the guy wasn't so laid back after all. He was glad to see it. His sister didn't need some pushover. Sitting his half-finished drink on a shelf, he took out his wallet, pulling out a business card before passing it over.

"It's impressive you're a manager in IT. Send me your resume later tonight."

Lawrence deposited the card in his own wallet without looking at it, before pulling out one of his own.

"Here you go, *my* card. You can feel free to look me up on LinkedIn."

Robert took it and put it in his back pocket. "No doubt, I will."

And he would, along with a full background check on the man as soon as Monday morning hit. Picking up his drink, Robert took a long sip and just stared at Lawrence. The guy coolly returned his gaze, making no move to talk into the silence. But Robert could tell by the stiff way he was holding himself that he wasn't completely at ease. His guard was up, waiting to see what would happen next...smart man.

"Didn't I hear you play pool? Want to go a round or two while I wait for my wife to cool down?"

"Sure, why not." Nodding his head slightly, Lawrence picked up his own glass needing a drink. "Maybe I'll have better luck with you than I did with your sister."

Robert shot him a genuine smile and laughed. "She kicked your ass, huh?"

"Something like that." Lawrence conceded, rubbing his chin thoughtfully. "You could say I got hoodwinked."

Nodding solemnly Robert proclaimed, "Women, will do that to you."

Chapter Sixteen

They left her brother's house a little after nine which meant it was pitch black. Brihanna rode with Lawrence home, since she had taken an Uber to Mika's house and wanted to spend the night at his place. But no matter how hard she tried, she couldn't get Lawrence to share what was said in the basement. Only that they'd played pool, had a conversation and a drink. While she had spent most of the time upstairs fretting, since Robert hadn't been exactly warm and welcoming during dinner.

Mika bless her heart, had tried to distract her. Instead, focusing on the fact their meal had been a success, and no one was heaving it up into the toilet. Eventually, they started planning what to cook for Thanksgiving and how they would surprise the rest of the family. The two ended up laughing with Mika vowing to get it on tape. Robert hadn't said anything to Brihanna before they left either, just looked at her oddly before giving a harder than usual hug. Currently irritated with her lack of success, Brihanna stopped pestering Lawrence for clues and went straight to the source.

Bri-Bri: So...what did you two talk about?
Robert: Something that's none of your business
Bri-Bri: You were extra quiet at dinner, that's not like you
Robert: I didn't have anything to say...at the time
Bri-Bri: Well...what do you think of Lawrence?

It took Robert so long to answer, she didn't think he would.

Robert: He's okay...not bad

Coming from anyone else that wouldn't be a ringing endorsement, and it wasn't in this case either. But from Robert it meant he didn't *hate* the man and found him tolerable. That was good enough for her.

Bri-Bri: *Cool because I like him*

Her brother didn't respond to that, and she hadn't expected him to. He had said his piece and so had she. The heavy dread of Robert disapproving of her "maybe" boyfriend dissipated, and she was able to tune into Lawrence more fully.

"Did you learn to cook for me?"

"Starting to think a lot of yourself, huh? I wouldn't say *for* you. I was just ready to learn."

"You sure you didn't do it for me...because that thought turns me on."

"I'm starting to think everything does." Brihanna grinned shaking her head.

"You may be right, or maybe it's anything *you* do."

Lawrence suddenly got over into the right lane, then a little ways up pulled into a dark empty parking lot of an old closed Kmart.

"Why are we stopping here? Is something wrong with the car?" Brihanna was ready to call her towing company.

"Nothing's wrong, I just think you deserve a reward for your efforts in the kitchen."

Looking out the window Brihanna pondered, "What reward would be here?"

"The one I'm about to give you." He reached over and undid her seat belt, then put her phone away. "Climb over in that back seat and spread your legs for me...I'll do the rest."

Brihanna's mouth worked but nothing came out. She hadn't made out in a parked car since she was seventeen, and that hadn't ended well. One of her cousins had recognized the car and put a stop to the party in her pants. But that was then, and this was now.

"Well, my mama always said achievements should be rewarded." Brihanna licked her lips in anticipation.

* * *

Returning from dropping Brihanna at home the next day, Lawrence did something he rarely did. Had a drink alone. He kept a small pack of beer in the fridge for when friends came over, but that often went months untouched. And he *never* had hard liquor in the house. If others brought drinks over, he made them take left-overs home. He'd had to dump a bottle or two down the drain when folks forgot. That act alone was considered a sin by most, you were never supposed to waste good liquor. Lawrence didn't care, he just never wanted it to be an easy option for him. But today he got comfortable with a beer and reflected on yesterday.

The dinner with her brother had been more stressful than he'd realized. It had been easy enough to ignore his hostility while in the presence of the women. Cold aggression is how Lawrence would describe it. The only other time he'd come up against the like was in boardrooms with VPs and CEOs. It was that unmistakable vibe they gave off, as if your very existence was annoying. Peering through you, as they devised a way to put you in your place. Lawrence ran into it enough at work to recognize it when he saw it.

By the time they reached the basement, Robert seemed more weary than vexed. Probably distracted by his wife being pissed at him. After the business card snipping episode, Robert had tried another tactic with him as they played pool. Pretending to be relaxed but not outright friendly, as he called himself giving tips on Brihanna. Sipping the brew he didn't even taste, Lawrence thought back on it.

"I'm not surprised you met Brihanna online, she's not really a people person. Doesn't like to go out much or party. A homebody, kinda boring."

"Your sister is the furthest thing from boring. I'm past the partying stage so it works for me." Lawrence said dryly.

"Huh, if you say so. What do you two sit at *home* doing?"

At the obvious ploy Lawrence grinned. Did the man think he was an idiot and would say "we sit at home fucking"? They did, but only a complete asshole would tell a woman's brother that. But he couldn't resist needling him, letting his smile turn a little lecherous before answering.

"Let's say we have a lot of interests in common. We don't have a problem staying, *active*."

Robert's eyes narrowed slightly before he shrugged.

"Enjoy it while it lasts. Brihanna never keeps her men around for long. She usually finds something lacking in them. She can be harsh and picky with exactly what she wants. Her cousins...there're four of them. You did know that, right?"

"Yeah, I've heard."

"Well, she may have gotten her over opinionated personality from all of us. She doesn't put up with shit if you get my drift. Not that we think she should. I'm just saying some men might find her difficult. At a minimum, difficult to keep her attention."

If Lawrence was holding his pool stick tight, that was to be expected as he tried not to get angry.

"Brihanna strikes me as a levelheaded woman. If she found something lacking in other dudes, there probably was. I don't find her overly picky at all, just a woman with standards that she sticks to. If she got her boldness and confidence from the men in her family, then I thank you for it. It's refreshing to see a woman who knows what she wants and who she is. Not afraid to be different."

Lawrence had been taking and dropping shots as he talked.

"As for the last. I won't be losing sleep over that. Real men, know how to keep a real woman's attention. I know what Brihanna likes."

He almost added *what she needs*, but was trying to leave the basement without coming to blows with her brother.

"Okay, whatever you say. I'm sure they all thought that. Anyway...Thanksgiving is around the corner. Should I expect you to be showing up at my house *again*? The entire family will be here."

"If Brihanna wants me there, then I'll be there."

Robert had dropped his interrogation, evaluation, hell whatever he called himself doing after that. And here it was a whole day later and the conversation still grated on Lawrence's nerves. It was obvious her brother had been trying to scare him off one way or the other, which was bullshit. There was nothing objectionable about him *or* Brihanna. He tried to remind himself he was dating the doted on, only female of a small, close family.

Finished with the beer, he was determined to let it go. It was over and done with and Brihanna seemed happy with the outcome. He should be focusing on the fact *she* liked what they had. *She* thought he was good enough and that was all that mattered.

* * *

Or so Lawrence thought, until he found himself agitated two weeks later at her house. It was the weekend before Thanksgiving and she had yet to ask him to her family dinner, even though the subject came up all the time. As Brihanna was excited about rubbing it in her family's face that she could cook an edible meal. If she wasn't making meal plans with her sister-in-law, she was testing dishes on him.

Her cooking was great, but he was starting to wonder if she was satisfied with *him*. Lawrence knew it was all in his head, but now he wondered if he hadn't passed the "test" after all? If he had, wouldn't she invite him to share the holiday with her? This was new territory for him.

He'd never been in the predicament of needing to gain acceptance from a woman's family, not unless you counted his senior prom date. For once he actually cared about making a good impression. His position after meeting Robert had only become firmer, he had no plans *not* to be in Brihanna's life. They were good together. It frustrated him that anyone in her family might be able to derail that.

Of course, he knew Brihanna had her own mind and a strong will, but he wasn't stupid or blind to human nature. Both men and women, who were super close to their families could *and* would let them interfere in relationships. Just like Robert had tried to put doubts in his head about her personality, he knew the man could whisper the same in Brihanna's ear about him if he wanted to.

Any of her cousins could probably do the same. He'd been around a few times when she was on the phone with Darrell. It was very clear they were tight, he bet the man's words carried weight. This was why Lawrence couldn't shake the feeling that he needed to show up and face them all.

Not in a truly confrontational way, but just showing up would let them know he was in her life and serious. Robert had basically thrown the challenge down by putting the question out there. If he didn't show up, Robert would assume Lawrence didn't want to face the scrutiny. So he decided to broach the topic with Brihanna, while trying not to come off weird.

"I was thinking you should come meet my family next week."

Brihanna swung around, trying to figure out had his mouth moved or was she hearing things. They were playing a two-player battle game and her character got hacked to death as she sat staring at him.

"Pause the game." She told him since he had the main controller. "Now say that again?"

"Do you want to meet my folks?" Putting the game aside, he turned to face her, trying to read her expression.

"I mean sure, I just...I have my family get together. I've never missed it."

"You won't have to miss it now. I've been thinking, we eat early around one or one thirty. We're pretty informal, extended family drop in and out, so it's never too large of a crowd at once. We can leave whenever you need to, so that we get to your brother's house in time. Didn't you say you guys don't eat until the game is over?"

"Yeah, I guess that could work." Brihanna leaned back running the scenario in her head. "Okay...the more I think about it the better it sounds!"

Lawrence was relieved. She wasn't averse to meeting his people, which he hadn't realized how much he wanted that. His cousins knew about her of course, almost from the start and had even met her once. His mother was a different story. He didn't talk to her about females, *ever*. They didn't have that kind of open relationship. Every once in a while, she joked that she was never getting grandkids and he'd reply, *definitely not this year.* But that was as close as they came to discussing his relationship status.

"Great, I'll let my mom know. You don't mind I'll be meeting the rest of your family, do you?"

At that Brihanna frowned a little.

"Of course not. I just hope they don't get on your nerves too bad, or for that matter mine. Just be warned, everyone is going to look at you like I brought a two headed unicorn home. I don't normally bring guys around. I apologize in advance for all the shenanigans. If you don't mind meeting all those crazy folks, then more power to you."

"I think I can handle myself."

"Don't say I didn't warn you. Anyway, this is perfect! I won't have to help or stand around as my aunt tells me I'm *not* helping. And it will make it easier for me to walk in at the last minute with a dish too."

Brihanna was up pacing.

"Oh wait, what does your mom like? Your uncle and your cousins? I can't show up without *something*. You write down a short list of things they like that no one else usually brings. I want to call Mika and see if she has any ideas!"

He laughed as she grabbed her phone, running into the kitchen. Then he found a notepad so he could do what she'd asked. He felt much better about the whole thing now. Like he'd told her, he was sure he could hold his own with her family while keeping his cool.

Chapter Seventeen

Brihanna timed it so they arrived at the house five minutes after the game ended. She was hoping everyone would be distracted with celebrating a rare Thanksgiving win from the Detroit Lions to pay her much attention. The decision to do desserts for both households had been easy, figuring on days like this you could never have too many. Her golden butter, chocolate four-layer cake with ganache drizzle was a hit at his mom's house. Fingers crossed it would be the same here.

That visit had gone well as far as Brihanna could tell. Lawrence mother seemed genuinely pleased to meet her, plying her with a big hug upon arrival. Then Brihanna had been introduced to Uncle Luc, and his wife Sandra. This time *she* was the one giving the hard hug. Of course, she didn't say anything, but she was so grateful for the man who had protected a young and emotionally hurt Lawrence.

His cousins had greeted her warmly too. Brihanna met them back in September when the group had an impromptu dinner. The feeling was mutual as she liked the pair. Just as Lawrence said, different members of his family dropped in for a plate and to hang out as the afternoon went on. There was a bit of curiosity about her presence as it seemed Lawrence had never brought a woman to a holiday gathering before, another thing they had in common.

But now it was time to deal with her own clan. Brihanna had told her mom she was visiting a friend's family and would be late. No one besides the hosts, knew she was bringing him. At least none that had heard it from her. Minutes before they pulled up, she texted Mika to come open the door.

"Hey Cutie!" Mika greeted Lawrence, as she ushered them in, taking coats.

"Thanks for allowing me back, I wasn't so sure after the last time."

"Don't thank me." Mika warned. "You still have to get through today." Turning to Brihanna she said, "Cute dress!"

Wanting to make a good impression on his family, Brihanna had donned a dress again. She was discovering that some of the looser fit ones were really comfortable. Her dress was black, decked with different colors and shaped leaves, with acorns sprinkled throughout. Paired with a pair of burgundy, wool leggings and ankle boots.

"Thanks. What's the mood?"

"You already know, everyone's happy including me about that win. Though Cam lost his random bet this year. Let's get your cake in the kitchen, your mom and aunt are putting the last touches on everything."

Lawrence took her hand and squeezed, taking a deep breath she led him forward to start the introductions. Her mother was outright shocked but recovered quickly, then had the same look on her face as *his* mother. Looking at it now Brihanna saw it was hope. Dang, had both women thought their kids were hopeless in the romance department? She had to hand it to Aunt D though. The woman didn't gush or say anything inappropriate. Instead, she gave him a polite greeting but behind his back she winked at Brihanna and gave her a thumbs-up. Both women so fascinated with Lawrence that neither asked about the cake.

Johanna ran her eyes over her daughter, trying her best to keep the excitement she was feeling off her face.

"You look lovely by the way. I really like that dress." Giving a gentle smile she waved the girl towards the loud living room. "Go on Brihanna, everyone is in there. Introduce your friend, then y'all wash up. Dinner will be ready in about five minutes."

Brihanna bit the bullet and went inside. At first no one seemed to notice her, until Mika opened her big mouth.

"Hey everybody, look who's here!"

When everyone turned, it was like a record skipped. The silence interrupted a few seconds later when one of the younger kids asked, "Who is he?"

"Hey guys, this is my man, um...friend Lawrence."

All the guys stood up. Her cousins, Cam, even her teenage second cousin. It wasn't until Mika pinched Robert that anyone spoke.

Sighing wearily, Robert made his way over, extending a hand.

"I see you made it...I was starting to wonder. Welcome."

Lawrence shook his hand but could tell Robert wasn't overjoyed to see him. Compared to a few of the other looks he was getting, he'd take it. Robert's welcome seemed to help break the tension in the room, as all the inflated chests subsided—*slightly.*

*

Lawrence was finally able to put names to the faces he'd heard so much about. Thomas and Edward seemed to get over his being there fairly quickly, though he saw them exchanging looks a few times after he commented on something. The younger two Devon and Darrell, not so much. But overall he hadn't been asked any prying questions, and the conversation flowed. Talk about the game dominated for a good while, before folks moved onto general topics. Until apparently he hit a nerve.

"Bri, let me get some more of that stuffed pasta." The comment made Mika beam and Devon grunt loudly with annoyance.

"You do know her name is Brihanna, right?"

Lawrence ignored the man and turned to Johanna instead.

"Ms. Johanna, Brihanna is a beautiful name. Did you know the root of her name means *strong* or *she ascends*?"

"Oh, that is lovely! I didn't know that when I picked it. Just thought it sounded pretty to be honest. Thank you for sharing that!"

That only earned Lawrence another dirty look. And he could have sworn he heard a muttered "kiss ass" too. Like all larger family gatherings, it was easy to see if they were close or had underlying tensions. *This* family was very comfortable with each other. Cracking jokes, debating with heat, yet everyone seemed to be in their element. That wasn't quite true, he noticed Edward's wife seemed extra quiet, distracted even.

It was clear the men were tight and embraced fully anyone else they considered family, like Robert's friend Cam. Halfway through dinner Thomas stood up and made a toast to Robert and Mika on their first-year anniversary taking place in two days. That opened the floodgates of congrats and teasing, and that told him this family loved each other as well.

They were in the middle of enjoying dessert and eating seconds, when he noticed Mika giving Brihanna a "look", which she then passed on to one of the teenagers, who nodded and picked up their phone. Lawrence wasn't surprised when he got a kick under the table, it was time for him to do his part.

"Everything was delicious ladies, well done."

"Thank you! We try our best. We love this crazy bunch." Johanna effused.

"We love you too, Aunt J." Edward assured her.

"What about me? Your own mama?" Dolores exclaimed.

"Yeah, we love you. We have too." Devon said to laughter.

When Lawrence got another kick, he cleared his throat. "That stuffed pasta was excellent. Which one of you ladies made that?"

"Oh that." Dolores waved her hand dismissively. "That's something Mika had catered. It was really good though."

Robert beat Mika to the punch. "Actually, *my* wife cooked that."

"Get out!" Johanna exclaimed pleased.

Dolores cackled. "Then shut the front door *and* the back!"

"Mika cooked this?" Darrell pointed his fork at the half devoured item on his plate. "Shi-I mean shoot, I need video proof."

Robert scowled. "I actually have that, she made me record it. My princess can cook." Smiling he leaned over giving her a kiss, before turning and pointing a finger towards Brihanna. "And believe it or not, that one made the chocolate cake."

If Lawrence had thought the announcement of Mika cooking had caused a ruckus, it was nothing compared to what happened next.

"Lawd Jesus!" Dolores shouted. "Miracles do happen."

"My prayers are answered!" Johanna praised.

All the cousins were scoffing with disbelief.

"Are we being invaded by aliens?" Devon puzzled. "What in the world is going on?"

"What the hell Dev? I have to be taken over by extraterrestrials to bake a cake?"

"Yes!"

"I think you killed it Baby Girl. Everyone at my mom's loved it! She wants me to ask you for the recipe."

His show of support didn't go over like he thought it would. Dolores slid down in the chair, clutching her chest. All the men stopped laughing and turned to eyeball him, *again*. Her mother looked like she had something in her eye she was blinking so fast.

"You baked his mama a cake?" Johanna tried to wrap her head around that.

"Did he just call her baby girl?" Thomas muttered. That didn't sit well with him. It was a nickname he and Edward had used affectionately since Brihanna was a teenager.

"Let's stay focused people." Andrea jumped in. "When in the world did you two learn to cook? And why am *I* just finding out about this?"

"Brihanna roped me into taking cooking classes with her back in August."

At Mika's explanation Johanna's hand went to her heart. "Brihanna *wanted* the classes?"

Robert saw how dark his sister's face was getting. He could tell it had nothing to do with embarrassment and was more about her rising temper. Deciding to put an end to this he declared.

"It doesn't matter. Both of you did an outstanding job. Now, somebody pass me a piece of that damn cake. I'm not missing out this time."

*

Brihanna was coming back from helping to put the food up, when she heard Edward asking a question she was not happy with.

"Lawrence, are you up for coming outside with the fellas for a drink? It's a little ritual we do."

"He isn't a big drinker, maybe he should pass on that." Brihanna hurriedly threw out an excuse to keep him from being alone with *all* of them.

"One won't hurt, not after all the food I've eaten today." Lawrence shrugged easily.

"Why don't we integrate this tradition, bring it into the 21st century." Mika suggested, "Like I tried to do a while back."

To which Robert narrowed his eyes and said, "Not happening."

Johanna decided to speak up before this turned into a bigger deal than it was. Besides, if Brihanna's "friend" was going to be in the picture for a while, he needed to be able to hold his own in this family.

"Girls, let them have their time. Come on in the kitchen, we have our own gathering. Trust me, the older you get the more you'll appreciate some time away from men."

The women followed the advice, Brihanna reluctantly allowing Andrea to drag her off. Though the men had barely settled down outside before Mika came out the door, wrapping a scarf around Robert's neck and giving him a kiss on the cheek, all while he rolled his eyes.

"What do you want Minx?"

"Me? Nothing! Just wanted to keep you warm and say that I didn't mean it about us crashing your boys' club."

"Oh, so now you're on my side?" Robert asked in surprise.

"I'm always on your side." Mika sounded hurt. "Well, wait...when it benefits me. Besides, I like being the only one who can ignore your rules."

Then she glanced at Lawrence. "Now, promise me you boys will play nice with your new friend."

Robert shook his head after looking at the stubborn expressions on his younger cousins faces, not to mention the more calculating looks on the older two.

"You know I don't make promises I can't be sure to keep."

"I know." Mika said easily. "However, now I can honestly say I tried. I was just doing a CMA. You know *covering my ass.*"

Walking inside she firmly shut the door, leaving the men to their own devices.

Seconds later, the interrogation started.

"Did you make her wear that dress?" Devon was leaning forward, his drink dangling from his hand.

"What?" Lawrence laughed until he saw no one else was. He thought the question was ridiculous.

"Of course not. I don't care what she wears. I'm not into fashion."

Darrell wasn't buying it. "Bri only wears dresses for weddings or funerals."

"Again, I don't care if she never wears them. I thought *you* were extra close to her? I would think you'd know her better. I don't get the sense that anyone forces her to do anything."

Normally, Cam wasn't an instigator, but he had reservations about this dude too. Brihanna was a sweetheart and he didn't want to see her get hurt.

"Damn, I think he just said you don't know your own cousin."

"That's what it sounds like to me." Devon didn't even try to hide his shrewd grin.

"I'd say there's nothing wrong with anyone's hearing." Lawrence confirmed.

Thomas chuckled at Lawrence's dig. "Got some balls on him, huh?"

"Oh, *I* know my cousin all right." Darrell said tightly. "And some of the shit I've heard tonight doesn't sound like her."

Lawrence bit his tongue to keep from saying something else scathing.

"Let me get this straight." Edward paused to take a long drink. "You don't think Bri doing two things she normally doesn't, has nothing to do with *you*? I was starting to think you were a smart man, but now..."

"The question I was asked was did I "make her" and the answer was I don't make Bri do anything. I couldn't care less what she wears." He resisted throwing in he preferred her without clothes. "I don't care if she can cook either. I'm a grown man, I know how to feed myself."

"Robert mentioned you two met online. How many women have you picked up using internet sites?"

Lawrence took Devon's measure at the question. *This* one was slick. He could imagine Devon coming at you from the front *or* the back. Whatever would accomplish his goal quicker.

"Probably less than you have."

Everyone but Devon and Darrell cracked up.

"Hell, he's got you there!" Thomas laughed out loud.

"I'm starting to like you." Cam raised his glass in Lawrence's direction.

Devon narrowed his eyes, shifting forward in his seat. "You got jokes, huh?"

"Naw, just answers to you all's intrusive, rude ass questions." Lawrence finally let some sharpness enter his tone.

"You seem to talk a lot of shit my man." Darrell was not amused.

"He's right." Robert spoke up for the first time. "We are some rude assholes, but Darrell's right too. You talk a lot of shit. You play ball?"

"Yeah, I play. Why?"

"Can you make a five-man crew?"

Lawrence wasn't sure where this was going, "I can make it happen."

"Tell you what. We'll call a truce the rest of the evening if you meet us on the court. Us, against your folks." Robert nodded around to his family. "We can do our shit talking there."

"Yeah...okay." There had to be a catch, and he didn't have time to guess. "What's the catch? I know you have one."

"See, told you he was smart-*ish*." Edward quipped.

Robert smiled slowly. "Nothing in life is free, not even a truce. Your team loses, *you* owe me five hundred dollars. We lose...which we won't, I owe you the same."

Lawrence took a sip, making it seem like he wasn't rushed or pressed by the challenge. But he just didn't have it in him to ignore this.

"Yeah, that works. You still have *my* card, get at me and we'll set it up."

Chapter Eighteen

A few weeks after the holiday Brihanna got a text from Mika about meeting for dinner earlier than normal. Arriving, there was another surprise when they entered the kitchen and she spotted Andrea.

"Hey, I didn't know you'd be here." She gave the woman a hug before sitting. "What are we doing, some kind of girls' day?"

"Yeah, I figured it had been awhile since the three of us got together." Mika blew on the steaming cup in front of her. "You don't mind do you?"

"Don't be stupid, of course not. This just made my day."

Brihanna barely had a beverage in her hand before Robert walked in carrying a small duffle bag. "Where are you off to Robert?"

"Out of this house, away from three troublemakers." Robert asserted, giving his wife a kiss before walking on.

"I resent that." Andrea said, before sipping her tea. "I'm as innocent as a newborn babe. Don't lump me in with these two."

"Shiidd...that ain't what Cam says." Robert yelled back.

"What!" Andrea sputtered.

Mika laughed and teased her bestie until she heard the garage door opening. Then, she turned nonchalantly to Brihanna.

"You know he's going to play that game with your man, right."

"Really?" It was her turn to look stupefied. "Lawrence didn't mention it, and I just spoke to him last night."

"Hmm, he didn't tell you that Robert roped him into playing at Thanksgiving?"

"Yeah, but not that they'd set a date."

"Yup." Mika slurped her coco. "*All* your cousins plus Robert and Cam are playing.

Brihanna had grown up seeing them play ball. They got physical and outright mean, and that was when they were playing with family members.

Brihanna moaned. "I have to tell him to cancel."

But when she reached for her cell on the counter, Mika swooped in and got it first.

"Nope. You can't tell a grown man he can't play ball."

"Yeah, what's the big deal?" Andrea was confused.

"You guys know why. If last month was bad you know this is going to be worse. You two haven't seen them play, they're all extra aggressive."

Andrea furrowed her brow, thinking about the time she had seen Robert and Cam box each other. Then she thought about the rest of the men. "You're right, that's not good."

"Exactly!" Brihanna lunged for her phone only to be swatted away. "Give me my phone, or tell me where they're playing at."

"No." Mika said calmly, licking the whipped cream off her lip. "What would you look like storming up there and trying to stop them? Lawrence's friends and family will be there. You'll embarrass him and everyone will think you're crazy."

"Then why did you even tell me?"

"I just thought you'd want to know." Mika hunched her shoulders. "Now if you ask nicely, maybe your favorite sister-in-law—"

"You're my only one." Brihanna cut her off. "Which I'm starting to regret."

"*Maybe* she and her best friend will go down there with you to watch them play. And help you *not* make a fool of yourself."

"Sure, I'll go." Andrea quickly agreed, sensing the younger woman's rising frustration. "I wouldn't mind watching the game."

"*I* wouldn't mind seeing all this aggression you think is going to happen. Stuff like that turns me on." Mika added.

"That's because you have a problem." Brihanna muttered.

"True." Mika jumped up. "I'm driving! Follow me upstairs so we can get ready."

"Ready for what?"

"Sometimes it's better not to even ask." Andrea advised. Patting the other woman on the back as she went to follow Mika.

* * *

"We look like idiots." Brihanna slammed out of Mika's car at the rec center.

"Speak for yourself." Andrea adjusted her long, cherry-red and black wig under her winter cap. They had quickly flat-twisted her hair down so it would fit. "I'm starting to like mine."

"Good for you. But you're not wearing a wig that was on your brother's wife's head when they had sex."

Brihanna referenced the short blond wig she wore.

134

"Don't worry so much about that." Mika waved the concern away. "By the time we got to the nitty-gritty he'd ripped that off."

"Thanks for that visual. This is stupid."

"Look." Mika swung around a few feet from the door. "Robert is not going to kill me for being here. Maybe you weren't supposed to know. I might have betrayed a marital trust, all for you!"

Andrea rolled her eyes at the dramatics but couldn't stop a snicker escaping.

"I'm also trying to stop you from losing your man." Mika continued. "If he finds out you're here undermining him..."

"I'm not-"

"You are." Mika cut her off. "I told you at the house, we had to disguise ourselves so none of the men would recognize us."

"Why couldn't we all just wear a hoodie like you?" Brihanna narrowed her eyes. "Or just a hat?"

"Because it's *your* family and *our* husbands. They would recognize us. Plus, we all couldn't walk in there with our hoodies pulled tight. We'd look like terrorists."

"We're half-way in the hood, no one would think that." Brihanna countered.

"Well...they might think we're in a gang. I just got my nails done, I can't fight this week."

Brihanna laughed at the absurdity that was Mika. "You make me *so* sick sometimes."

"Aww, I love you too Sis!"

Brihanna shook her head, the crazy woman probably just wanted to pretend they were on an undercover sting like Charlie's Angels.

The women made their way inside the gymnasium, taking seats high up in the stands, close to the door. There was a pretty decent crowd of spectators and waiting players. They asked someone next to them how long the game had been going, and were told a little less than ten minutes. Brihanna pointed out Lawrence's cousins Mike and Malcolm to the girls. She also recognized Jarod from photos Lawrence had showed her on Facebook. However, she wasn't sure who their fifth team member was.

The opposing team of course was her family. Robert was the power forward while Edward played the small forward. Devon was the center and Cam was the point guard. Darrell rounded them out as the shot guard. It seemed like Thomas was acting as referee. Thank God, she could always count on him to be sensible. He probably recognized it was about to be an intense game, and it was.

They were playing full court having paid for a full hour slot. The rec made money that way. Having certain times available to buy and other times free and open to all. The first game ended with Robert's team getting to fifteen first. They had a three minute break and then Thomas was doing another tip off. Brihanna figured they were playing the best of three to fifteen. Which meant if her brother's team won the next game they were done, but it could potentially go to the third one.

Brihanna had sat on the sidelines of a number of pickup games growing up, so knew a few basics. People played by all kinds of different rules. This second round it seemed Lawrence's team had gotten the lay of the land. Mainly, that her family played fast and mean. This time they came out swinging, literally, elbows thrown all over the place, from faces to guts. All three women winced when Devon blocked a ball and sent it directly into Jarod's face.

"Dang, that had to hurt." Andrea stated the obvious.

A few minutes later Mike pushed Darrell hard enough for him to fall while guarding him during a pass. When he jumped back up, a chest bumping and shoving match started. Thankfully, no one else from either team joined in as Thomas broke it up quickly.

"I can't watch this." Brihanna briefly covered her face.

"It's not that bad." Mika tried to sound like she believed it. "They're just being guys, rough housing it."

"I don't know. It does seem a little rougher than it needs to be. Oww!" Andrea exclaimed after Mika stepped on her foot. "What? I was just being honest."

"But *not* helpful." Mika hissed in her direction.

"I'm not blind, she's right. I can see they're being assholes, to Lawrence in particular. I'm sure *everyone* can see it."

"Well...it's because he's a really good player. He's holding his own, see look at him." Mika pointed back to the game.

Snapping around Brihanna saw he was in a scrimmage with Devon for a rebound. Devon ended up on the ground and Lawrence made the basket.

"I'm glad he ended up on his ass." Brihanna sneered. "He's been the worst by far."

"You see how blood thirsty she is over her man Andrea? Isn't it cute!"

"Shut up Mika, I'm not in the mood for jokes."

"I wasn't joking. You are *fierce*. If your family could see your face, they'd leave your man alone."

Brihanna didn't respond, just watched the game. It was hard fought, but Lawrence's team won the second game to tie it up. After another small break the third game started. It was obvious everyone was tired. She could see the only thing keeping them going was the drive to take home the win.

This game had worked her nerves, she felt helpless that Lawrence had to endure this because of her. This wasn't a friendly "let's just hang out" game between men who recently met. They saw a man who'd managed to get close to her, and they didn't like it. She was furious at her family for taking their over protectiveness this far! She wasn't some princess in a tower and Lawrence didn't have to slay dragons to prove himself worthy.

Their behavior was idiotic, patronizing and sexist. She was mad at Lawrence for agreeing to this game as well. It was no mistake he hadn't mentioned the game last night. Men and their weird pride, she would never understand it. Right now, she wanted to smash all their heads together. At this point she didn't even want to be here anymore.

As if she could read Brihanna's mind Mika said, "Hey, we should probably go, the games almost over. We want to make sure we beat them back to the house."

"Fine by me." Brihanna was more than ready to go.

Chapter Nineteen

Lawrence opened the door to his home worn out. After quickly changing out of his jeans to something looser, he made his way to the living room and eased down on the sofa. He hadn't played that rough of a b-ball game since college, when he'd been in much better shape. He closed his eyes and replayed the game in his mind.

They had started a bit late as the last game wrapped up but not by much. Lawrence met her family on the side of the court, expecting to see the same glowers from Thanksgiving. Instead, they'd all been smiling, though not that pleasantly. After introductions everyone got right to it. The game had been hard and fast out the gate, *and* physical. Elbows were thrown and shoulder checks were aplenty. Pretty much everyone on the court met the floor at least once if not more. Not surprisingly, he'd had more than his fair share. They'd definitely had it in for him.

Honestly it had pissed him off, bringing out his competitive side. It didn't take long for him and his crew to start hitting back just as hard. In the end, it had been an intense, close game. True he'd ultimately lost, with the other team winning the last game by two points, but they'd made those bastards work for it. When they were shaking hands after the game, he'd made his way over to Robert.

"I got your money in the locker room."

"Save it." Robert shrugged, hands on his hips while he caught his breath. "We'll call it even if you buy us something to eat and a few drinks, after we hit the showers. That work for you?"

"I bet y'all asses, are going to eat a lot. But I suppose I'll save maybe fifty bucks."

The other man hadn't cracked a smile at his joke. Instead Robert looked at him in that way he had, as if he was trying to look through you then nodded once. Said "not bad" in his direction and walked away. Seconds later he'd felt an entirely too hard slap on his back as Darrell walked by.

"He must like you. Robert never misses a chance to take cash."

On his other side, Devon walked past giving another excessively hard hit before adding his two cents.

"I wouldn't say *like*, but maybe he doesn't hate you. *I'm* still making up my mind."

In the shower he had reminded himself his baby girl had her own mind and strong personality. Because if she was the type to let her family's approval dictate who she dated, he would be hit. The group ended up going to a local place not far up the road and after snagging two tables, ordered. It had turned into over an hour filled with trash talk and laughs, he'd been surprised. Afterwards he had limped his way home tired as hell.

Brihanna had told him almost since they met, that she had a very protective family. Even so, he figured she really meant her brother. Apparently not, and now his back and knee were paying for it. The sibling dynamic was something he wasn't familiar with. All her cousins seemed to treat her just like a younger sister. That he understood, as you could become very close to cousins you grew up with. You protected your tribe.

He wished he could have explained to the men he had no intentions of hurting Brihanna, at least not on purpose. That in fact he was coming to think of protecting her as *his* job. But men didn't go around talking to other men about stuff like that. Especially, men you didn't know well. All Lawrence could do was hope over time his actions would be enough to show them how he really felt. Until then her family would just have to deal with it. He'd proven today that he wasn't a pushover and wasn't going anywhere.

* * *

Immediately after getting back to Mika's house, Brihanna headed home. Having no plans to go back out either. That was until she got a text, over two hours after leaving the gym.

Mika: How's your man?
Bri-Bri: I don't know, haven't spoken to him
Mika: Mine came back a little beat up
Mika: He said yours was limping
Bri-Bri: That's what he gets, they all should suffer
Mika: Of course they should! Anyway... just FYI, later

"Shit."

Brihanna honestly didn't *want* to care that he was hurt. She was still mad he'd kept the game from her. If he was at home suffering that was his problem. And yet, ten minutes later on an annoyed sigh, she got up to pack a few things and left the house. When she got closer to his home she sent him a message.

Bri-Bri: Bored, headed your way to chill hope you don't mind?
Lawrence: No prob

Knowing what condition he was in, she wasn't surprised when he took a long time answering the door.

"Hey, sorry I texted last minute about coming over."

Lawrence waved away her apology. "Come on in."

After stepping out of her boots, she followed him as he slightly hobbled back to the couch. Watching as he gingerly laid down.

"What happened to you?"

"That basketball game with your brother was today."

"Oh, really?" Brihanna feigned surprise. "How did it go?"

Lawrence didn't answer right away, watching her take off the winter gear she wore. Noticing for the first time a small brown bag in her hand.

"It was brutal actually. We lost by two and I banged up my knee a bit. Didn't even start feeling it until I left the restaurant."

"Hmm, is it bad?"

"No. I'll just be a little sore and stiff, today and tomorrow. I've been icing it since I got home, on and off."

"Men...always downplaying injuries. I brought something that should make you feel better. Take off your shirt."

Frowning a little Lawrence did what he was told, handing it to her.

"How did you know I might need anything?"

"A little sly fox told me. Mika said Robert came home banged up, I figured that meant you might be as well."

"I won't turn down any assistance at this point."

"Sit up."

When he did, she squeezed behind him, unscrewing the top off the small jar.

"What exactly is in it?" Lawrence wrinkled his nose. Whatever it was, didn't smell like any ointment he'd used before.

"Not much. Some pepper, ginger, peppermint and mustard oil, then they mix it with shea butter. It's called African lion mustard rub. I picked it up from a tiny shop downtown."

"Does it actually work?"

"Yep, I've used it a few times. It helps drive blood flow, which helps with pain and soreness. Now be quiet while I work."

He shut up as Brihanna spread small amounts over his back, rubbing it in. She could see a dark bruise on one side of his shoulder blooming. When she finished with the ointment she went on to give him a light massage, being careful not to press hard.

"That feels good. Even that stuff you used...it's tingling." Lawrence eyes closed as she worked.

"I'm glad."

And she was, even upset she didn't want him hurt. Using the pads of her fingers to massage the sides of his neck, she pressed close to place an innocent kiss to his clean skin. Then Brihanna stopped abruptly, shifted and got up.

"Now let me take a look at this leg." Kneeling next to him she probed around. "This isn't good. You should have wrapped it. That would have kept the swelling down. Do you have anything I can use?"

"I probably have something, check the hallway closet with the towels."

While she ran to get that, Lawrence couldn't help but grin. He had been content to tend to himself, but it was nice to have her here fussing over him. Felt good to know she cared. When he heard her coming back, he wiped the smile off his face.

"Found it!"

Kneeling again, she started spreading a thick layer of cream around the entire puffed up area of his knee.

"Thanks for coming over and doctoring me. I seriously feel better already."

"I went back and forth on coming or not. But figured it was the least I could do since my family hemmed you up."

"This is true." Lawrence teased.

Brihanna felt his hand stroking the back of her neck as she started wrapping his leg. Thirty seconds later she fastened the wrap securely and looked his way.

"I'm glad I cut my hair before I met you. I bet you would be a puller. I had a guy do that once and I hit the shit out of him."

"If *I* pulled your hair...you'd like it."

"I have a feeling I would. Are you hurting anywhere else you want me to take a look at?" She sat back wiping her hands with a rag.

"I'm good, this was great."

"Are you sure nothing else needs tending?"

She ran her hand up his thighs and started massaging his package. That got his drooping eyes snapping back up.

"I mean...I guess I'm starting to feel an ache right where your hand is. But I don't think you should use that stuff on it."

"I can think of another way to get blood flow to this part of the body." Brihanna promised.

Pulling down his shorts, being careful of his knee, she stroked him to firmness, before taking him in her mouth. She worked him slow to start, then put a little more energy into it. Twisting her hands, sucking firmly with her wet mouth. It didn't take long before he was gripping the back of her neck.

"Damn Bri, you got me hot and bothered and I can't do anything about it."

"Who said you need to?"

Yanking off her fluffy, fuchsia sweater, she revealed she wasn't wearing a bra underneath. Brihanna stood so she could shimmy the loose fit jeans down her legs, her panties quick to follow.

"You killing me *Bri*. I don't think my knee will let me put it down like normal."

"Like I said, you don't have to." A quick dig in her pants pocket produced a condom which she flashed in his face. "Today, I get to be in control. Think you can handle that?"

"I hope so, because you have me at your mercy Baby Girl."

He watched as she carefully tore the packet, before putting the latex on his manhood.

"Why am I starting to think you came over here to seduce me, instead of heal me?"

Watching out for his leg, she sat over his lap, then came down on his shaft. Seating herself fully before answering.

"Why can't they be one in the same?" Brihanna started riding his length, thrilling in watching his eyes cross with pleasure. "Haven't you heard of sexual healing?"

Chapter Twenty

In the blink of an eye the craziness of the Christmas season was upon them. Robert and Mika had delayed officially celebrating their anniversary last month, but took a trip for the current holiday instead. Brihanna spent the majority of Christmas Eve with Lawrence at her place. Instead of either of them cooking they ordered via DoorDash from P.F. Chang's and decided to watch Christmas comedies only. None of that tearjerker stuff for them.

They made a deal to give one gift each, and it had to be something fun. He wanted to wait until midnight before exchanging presents, but she was able to wheedle it down to ten p.m. instead. After passing over the gifts, she was unreasonably pleased to see he'd wrapped it instead of using a bag. She loved ripping open things! Funny enough their boxes were near the same shape. Well, except the one she got was about three times thicker than the one handed to him.

Lawrence told her to go first and Brihanna let out a small squeal as she saw an Oculus Go, VR set.

"Oh, my god! Thank you Lawrence!"

"No problem. I just couldn't let you continue to go without one."

"They are so expensive! All the ones everyone recommended were $400 plus."

"They didn't do enough research." Lawrence shook his head. "There are some good quality ones way below that. I only paid about $170."

"That's not too bad at all! Okay, tell me about the specs. I know you looked them up."

"Of course I did, this model is pretty dope. It's wireless, built-in speakers and mic. It's good for gaming, but figured you'd like the entertainment and social aspects of it too. You can make what they call Oculus rooms to create a virtual apartment and invite up to three friends. Then play games, watch movies or share videos. I figured you could use that feature with me and your girls."

"I can't wait to use it!"

Lawrence chuckled, he loved seeing her excited. The thought of getting her one had been floating around since finding out she didn't own one. She gamed enough that he thought it was a good investment. Besides there were all kinds of ways you could use VR for relaxation or learning purposes. Like taking a skydiving jump while sitting in the comfort of your own home.

"I'll set it up for you. So you can try it out tonight."

"Great! But after you open your gift. I was thinking along the same lines in something we could share and use together sometimes."

Lawrence tore open the wrapping much slower than she had. In fact, he planned to keep it but didn't tell her that. Even here Brihanna couldn't help displaying her creative side. Somehow, she had bought custom wrapping paper. One of the pictures of them together from Comic-Con decorated it, with speech bubbles that said, "Merry Christmas" every few inches.

Grinning at the personality she put into even little things, his smile only broadened when he saw what she'd gotten him. Tom Clancy's *The Division 2* game. A role playing game, based on a more realistic doomsday army-government plot. It was one of the hottest games out this year. Beneath that was *Devil May Cry 5,* one of his favorite series.

"Hey! You remembered when I offhandedly mentioned wanting *The Division*? That was months ago."

"Yeah," Brihanna nodded like it was no big deal. "I know how much you like the realistic ones. You like to use that over analytical brain of yours."

"This is awesome, thanks. And *Devil May Cry* just came out two weeks ago. I forgot about the release and they were sold out when I checked a couple days back."

"It pays to think ahead." Brihanna smirked. "I bought it on pre-order over a month ago. I figured if you already had it you could exchange it for something else. But I know how much you love that stupid game."

"Look now, don't ruin my mood by talking trash about one of my top ten games."

"In the spirit of Christmas, I'll stop. I'm just glad you like your presents."

"You know I do. Thanks Bri. Now hand over your headset. Let's get this bad boy up and running."

* * *

Way before Valentine's Day became a reality, she told Lawrence she didn't want to do gifts. He nodded and said "okay" and went back to watching TV, which made her relieved that he hadn't assumed it was some female reverse psychology trick. Hadn't asked her fifty times if she was "sure" either, like she didn't know her own mind.

He did asked her later if she wanted him to make dinner reservations somewhere, but she'd declined that too, knowing neither of them would really enjoy the bustle of the crowded restaurants. So instead she suggested they cook in and relax at home. Brihanna planned to come by his place after work Friday, fill his stomach with great food, and then have hot sex all night. That was *her* version of a great V-day celebration. They ended up cooking together, and after clearing away the dishes, moved into the living room where she slid him a card.

"It's not a gift." Brihanna insisted. "Just a silly card."

Lawrence pulled it out and started cracking up before he even opened it. An old-fashioned, bulky computer was on the front, with the back of the UPC tower taken off. Tools and bolts strewn around it. Inside it read:

Thanks for making my circuits fire every single time.
Happy Valentine's Day

Below that was a personal message that read, "*I enjoy every minute, hour and week I spend with you. Yours, Bri*".

"This isn't silly, I like it. It's clever and sweet. Thank you."

The soft look he sent her way, made her feel appreciated.

"I have something to give you too." Lawrence rose.

"It better not be a gift."

He only shrugged. "Stay there, you'll have to wait and see."

Returning from his second bedroom, Lawrence held what looked like one big box of heart-shaped chocolates.

"This is for you. Happy Valentine's day Bri."

Putting the candy box aside revealed a medium, rectangular box wrapped in the same paper she had used for his Christmas gift. Seeing it made her eyes unexpectedly tear up. She had to blink fast to stop the madness, even as she caressed the paper a few times. Instead of admonishing him for the gift, she looked over and said a simple "thank you".

Lawrence cleared his throat. "You don't know what it is yet, open it."

She did, only to find a jewelry box. Snapping the top open, she shifted through the tissue paper to view what was inside.

"Law...these are beautiful."

She lifted one silver hammered cuff bracelet and saw it had an "Argentium Silver" certification stamp on it. The other had an inscription:

Nubia

My only Wonder Woman

Law

Reading it had her eyes snapping up.

"I don't know what to say." Her voice was whisper thin with emotion. "I love them."

"Then that's enough. Come here and let me put them on."

Brihanna scooted closer, rolling up the loose sleeves of her tunic. The metal was cool against her skin and the fit was just right.

Lawrence kissed her forehead, surprised at how nervous he had been about this gift. But the awe in her eyes made the few hundred dollars he'd spent worth it. Seeing them on her wrists oddly made him feel *centered*. They also made a spark of desire light in his belly.

"They look good on you."

Lawrence's voice dropped to that octave that told Brihanna he was aroused. He slowly rubbed his thumb, back and forth across the fast pulse at her wrist.

"I'd like to see you with nothing on but these bands. Will you do that for me Brihanna?"

There was nothing unusual about his request for her to undress and she complied, making sure not to rush as she knew he liked the reveal. Blushing out of his sight when she made sure he saw the back of her bright, red V-day undies that said, "love me" before taking them off. Naked, she moved over to him, but he gently pushed her to the other end of the sofa.

"Sit over there and touch yourself."

Now *that* was a new request.

"I don't think I can." While he watched her undress all the time, usually she ended up touching him almost immediately or vice versa.

"Come on, Nubia wouldn't be so shy." He tried to coax, but when she only narrowed her eyes he tried another tactic, more playful. "If you want what I've got, you'll do it Bri."

Brihanna thought about ignoring his taunt. But looking at the bulge he was massaging through his pants she had to admit she *did* want what he had. *A lot.*

"Okay fine, but I want *you* naked too. I'm going to need visual stimulation for this."

Nodding, he efficiently undressed before sitting back on his side, his cock already half erect.

"Okay Baby Girl you're up."

Grabbing a throw pillow she put it behind her back, before slowly letting her legs fall apart. Brihanna used her grown-out hair to cover her heated face. She knew he wanted her to touch herself, but she couldn't yet. Masturbating wasn't the issue, him watching her so brazenly was. So she glided her hands up and down the middle of her thighs a few times before looking up. His eyes were caressing her skin, hungrily taking her body in, did turn her on. Seeing his need caged and waiting to get out was usually enough to make her wet, and it didn't disappoint now.

Gliding her hands to the top of her thighs she leaned forward, sliding her palms up and over her spread knees, down to her shins. Before circling her ankles with her fingers, as her breasts hung in the gap her legs created. Her shiny new bracelets winked against her skin and had Lawrence touching himself. Brihanna cupped the underside of her breasts, squeezing until her size 38B's jutted out.

Rubbing her areolas until the skin puckered into hardened nipples, she plucked at the points and Lawrence eyes watched every move like a hawk. His hand stroked lightly up and down his shaft. Brihanna gazed at his manhood, this part of him that brought her so much pleasure *and* tested her limits, connecting them physically.

There it was—that throb in her core which incited her fingers to slide on either side of her clit. While her eyes widened at the contact, his lowered. And she saw his breathing, not to mention his hand speed up. When she curled two fingers down and into her body, Lawrence closed his eyes as a tremor shook him.

When he opened them, it was to see her running the slickness from her fingers over her clit. Hearing her moan at the sensation had him choking on his own groan. Especially when the folds of her pussy were opened with her outside fingers, while she rubbed that wonderful nub of pleasure with the middle one.

"God Bri, you are so fucking beautiful."

She felt intoxicated by his words, moving her free hand to a breast. Silence descended, save for their heavy breathing and before long she was dipping her fingers in that honeypot of hers over and over, her thumb flashing across her clit from time to time. Lawrence was full out masturbating by now as well. Only when her hands became unsteady and her breath started to hitch did she speak.

"This was better than I thought it would be Law…"

Trailing off as she got distracted watching him spread pre-cum on the head of his penis. Licking her lips in longing before remembering the rest of her thought, she went on.

"But if *you* want what I've got, you better get over here and take it. If I make myself come...I'm done for the night."

"When you put it that way, it's time for me to go from watcher to participant."

Lawrence sprang at her, coming between her thighs, pulling her close for a sizzling kiss. Brihanna adapted quickly, pulling him closer by the back of his hips, nails digging in as she arched her back, her breasts pressed tight against his hard chest. In his own passion he half lifted her up, and Brihanna took the chance to wrap her legs around his waist, impaling his shaft in her heat. At the feel of her hot, silky walls clutching at him, he stilled in shock, his own body trembling as she began to pump against him.

Lawrence snapped.

Letting out a loud groan in the crook of her neck, he started meeting her thrust for thrust, pressing her down and into the cushions. They went wild for each other! Hands gripped, groped and grabbed, anything to get closer while their bodies strained to disappear within the other. All the while they kissed, licked and nipped wanting to consume their lover in every way possible. Her bracelets came off, each at different points in their frenzied love making, but *they* never parted. He stayed inside her warmth, as she clung to his steel, like her life depended on it.

Chapter Twenty-One

At some point during their frantic coupling, the two ended up on the floor. They were still there breathing heavily, her legs still wrapped around his body until he turned on his side. Silence descended on the room, until Lawrence spoke up with worry in his voice.

"We didn't use a condom." Lawrence spoke in belated dismay.

Brihanna was acutely aware they hadn't, she could feel his warm semen on her thigh. It was a novel experience, as he was the first man to leave his seed inside her. Sitting up she leaned over his chest so they could face each other.

"Law, I really liked what we just did, *how* we did it. It was wild, just us letting go. I want to do this more often."

He scowled. "Yeah wild, which is why we forgot birth control. We-"

Brihanna placed a finger against his lips.

"Which won't happen again. I want to do this from time to time, condoms included of course. I'm not saying I don't like how we normally get down. You know I love it, but I want to be able to do something different as well. Didn't you like it?"

"Are you crazy? Of course I did!" Shit, if it got any better he'd be passed out.

"Then it's settled?"

"Fine, you like it I love it. It's not like it was a hardship."

"Good!" She hadn't been sure he would be flexible with his sexual needs. "We should probably get off this floor."

"Hold on another minute." Lawrence pulled her back. "What do you think about hosting a small get together with me, here next month? Nothing fancy. A few of my friends, a few of yours, maybe some gamers? A little something to kick-off spring."

"That sounds cool, of course I'll come."

"No, I want us to throw it together. I want it to be *our* party."

"Oh." Brihanna sat up, putting her back against the couch and arms around her knees. "Like a couple's thing."

"Yeah, a couple's thing." Propping up on an elbow, he explained, "The thing that we are."

"Are we? I mean we're titling this now?"

"Don't you think it's about time Bri? We've been doing the "try" thing for over eight months. I think it's time to *buy*. To my mind, you're my woman and I don't mind people knowing it. Now, if I'm alone on that feeling just tell me. I get that we may have different thoughts on this."

"I didn't imagine us having this conversation naked for one thing, so allow me a minute. I don't have a problem with us being a couple. Hell Lawrence, I stopped fighting it before December was out! I deactivated all my dating sites. And just so we're clear, I haven't chatted, talked to or went out with anyone else since last July. This is just unexpected, plus I thought you weren't looking for a girlfriend when we met."

"I wasn't at that *exact* moment. But when people date long term eventually, unless they are both wasting time they'll get to this point. You're my baby girl. I like us together, on every level."

"I do too." Brihanna fluttered her lashes down, feeling modest yet happy at the same time.

Grabbing her hand Lawrence asked, "So you want to throw this party together or what?"

"Yeah, let's do it."

* * *

It took a little convincing, but they agreed to throw a St. Patrick's Day party. Lawrence had been apprehensive due to the level of drinking involved. But she reminded him he didn't have to drink at all, or they could both be designated sober people for the night. They could also encourage everyone to take a Lyft or Uber to the house instead of driving. They'd already decided they had plenty of room for people to squat overnight if they wanted.

Lawrence had a full finished basement, a second large bedroom, the living room and a small den people could lay out in. The only place off limits would be the main bedroom. It would be BYOB, though of course they would be providing food and basic drinks. It would be a great test for her cooking skills as well. She was happy about the general plans for the event but stressed by it nevertheless.

Since the holiday fell on a Tuesday, they decided to hold the party the Saturday beforehand, which meant they only had a month to put this together. Lawrence being a man didn't think it required much effort. He wanted to text folks a week beforehand and call it a day. Brihanna was by no means what you would call a "Suzy Homemaker", but even she knew you needed a tad more than that. In fact, she started shopping for decorations the next day. For once, happy that stores never waited for one holiday to end before putting out items for the next.

She made him do an on the fly guestimate of who to invite, reminding him he wanted to keep it small. He decided on his cousins, Jarod, two past co-workers around his age and one counterpart at his current job he trusted enough to party with. For her part, Dare and Dev were invited, three of her co-workers who she knew liked to game, and her two best friends. Speaking of her besties they had really stepped up. They'd been helpful when she was whining about being a little anxious at putting together her first formal gathering.

"Lawrence feels I'm overthinking everything." Brihanna complained as they sat around her living room the weekend after V-day.

"Well, are you?"

"I don't think so Tina. This is also our official coming out as a couple. It has a theme so it's a "hosted" party. Otherwise, it would just be a random get together."

"I agree." Danielle was painting her toes. "This matters, which is why he asked you to do it with him. You guys are making a statement in front of friends and family and whoever you consider important that you're a unit."

"Great, when *you* say it, it sounds even more serious. It's three weeks away, I still have to figure out the food!"

"Look, don't worry we'll help." Tina grabbed the notepad on the table. "Frankly, I think you should buy everything instead of cooking. Some quality frozen pizzas which you're an expert in, and some bulk wings from Sam's Club. Maybe a few meatballs if you want. The rest is easy. Buy some chips, salsa, a few cases of pop and water for those not drinking and you're done! I still have a brand-new gallon of martini mix, we can make virgin versions of those too."

"What about the vegetarian folks?" Danielle reminded them.

"Fuck 'em." They laughed as Tina rarely cursed. "No, I'm serious. We'll have one large fruit and veggie tray. When you do the evite you can note anyone with special dietary needs is free to bring their own food. Matter of fact, sneak in a general *you don't need to bring anything, but if you choose to, feel free.*"

"Actually, that sounds like a good idea." Brihanna was feeling better already.

"What are you guys doing for entertainment?"

"You mean besides drinking?"

Danielle snorted, "Yeah, besides that."

"Lawrence has a tricked out multi-player game system in the basement, and I've told you he has music hooked up throughout the house, so there's that." Trust Danielle to point out a problem. "Cards or whatever, you know the usual."

"Add that to the evite as well. Tell folks they're free to bring their favorite games or activity."

"Hot damn Tina, you got all the answers tonight!" Brihanna grabbed the notepad and wrote it down."

"Wait a minute." Danielle interjected. "How many folks are invited? Maybe you won't even need all that."

"Ummm, thirteen before counting ourselves."

Danielle frowned. "Are you letting people bring a guest or spouse?"

"Shit." Brihanna looked at Tina who just pointed at the notepad. "I know, I know. Add it to the evite."

* * *

With the help of her friends the work she needed to do for the party had been minimal. A little grocery shopping and her only other main duties became decorating and sending out the email. Oh, and reminding Lawrence to tell his friends directly about it to be on the safe side. The party was from six until whenever, so by 5:50 Brihanna was dressed and putting the first of the food in the oven. She was timing it so it would be ready in the next thirty minutes. Not sure if Lawrence's friends would be timely or not, but her girls had promised to be at least. When Lawrence came up behind her kissing her neck, she turned to give him a quick peck on the mouth.

"You look nice Bri, but you always do."

"Thanks. I was trying for a relaxed look but also something that says *fun*."

Brihanna had on a black and white, fitted Mickey Mouse off-the-shoulder jumper. Her hair worn in loose waves now that it was almost bra-strap length. The outfit was new, but the small pair of white Mickey earrings were something she'd had for years.

"I think you hit your mark." He gave her a distracted pat on the behind as he grabbed a water. "I'm hungry."

"You can't eat anything until the first guests arrive, so you better hope someone is on time."

They heard a knock on the door five minutes later.

Brihanna turned to him grinning. "Looks like you're in luck."

*

By the time she opened the door for Darrell and Devon at seven; Tina, Jarod, Mike, Samantha, Danielle, Malcolm and his date Brenda were already there.

"Hey! Thank you guys for coming."

"Like I would miss a chance to find out where *he* lives." Devon said after giving her a hug. "Bri, this is Jordan a friend of mine. Jordan this is my cousin."

"Nice to meet you Jordan. Feel free to take your coats off and relax. The closet is to your left."

She wasn't surprised Dev had brought a date. After the pair walked away, she teased Darrell.

"No date for you Dare?"

"No. Y'all can have this love crap. Did you hear what Robert did?"

Brihanna outright laughed. "Yeah, I heard. Crazy."

"Right? He's buying critters and you're hosting parties. The world is upside down."

"*Heeyyy, Dare.*" Danielle greeted, as they entered the living room.

"My night just got better." Suddenly his frown was turned upside down, as his eyes followed her.

"Try to behave Darrell. Some of my co-workers are coming tonight."

"It's a St. Patrick's Day party Bri. There is no behaving."

She waved him away to go open the door again, where she found a very pretty woman who looked half Japanese and black on the doorstep.

"Hi, I'm Julian, a friend of Lawrence."

That caused Brihanna's eyebrow to raise. Lawrence had given her everyone's name and email addresses. Brihanna had assumed that Julian was a guy, not a hot female about her height.

"Hey Jules!"

Brihanna stood back as Lawrence came up, watching the two hug. Now call her paranoid, but she thought there was more than friendliness flashing across the woman's eyes. Brihanna let it go, but knew who she'd be keeping a close eye on tonight.

Chapter Twenty-Two

By seven-thirty everyone had arrived, and the house was looking like the United Nations. On Lawrence's side you had Matthew and his wife Teresa who were white and Ken another work friend who was Filipino, not to mention the overly friendly Julian who she met earlier. Samantha was Brihanna's white coworker who was hella cool. Sometimes they went to the movies together, watching stuff no one else wanted to see. Lucus and his fiancé Valeria were Hispanic, the two had been tight since she first started at the company. Jennifer, her black counterpart at the job rounded out the gathering.

All in all, they ended up with nineteen people milling around. Most everyone brought some kind of a liquor, so they didn't have a worry there. True to her word, Tina whipped up her martini mix and they'd been drinking those since she arrived. Brihanna was limiting herself to one drink an hour max and no straight hard liquor. Some folks had board games, and Samantha bless her heart, walked in with a sampler of cheesecake.

In fact, she was eating some homemade queso dip that Valeria made, which showed how much she trusted Lucus to eat his fiancé's food when she didn't know the lady. Brihanna was having fun, and thought it was going rather well. Lawrence had one of his many playlists going and she and the rest of the ladies where in the living room, gossiping and dancing whenever a jam came on. That was until eight hit and

Lawrence asked if anyone wanted to play rise and fly Resident Evil.

"I'm in!" Julian announced running over to join him.

"Me too." Dare spoke up. "I want to get a look at this system Bri keeps telling me about."

"Cuz, break out some cards before you go." Malcolm told Lawrence. "We can play spades up here."

"I'll get them." Brihanna volunteered. "Head on downstairs."

"Are you coming?" Lawrence asked her.

"Not right now, but yeah I'll be down."

So Matthew, Lucus, Jennifer and Ken, followed the others downstairs. Malcolm and Devon started a rise and fly game of spades with their dates, with Jarod and Mike waiting in the wings for a turn. Brihanna was relieved to see everyone mixing, his friends with hers and vice versa. For a group where half the folks were sliding towards introverts, she was proud of everyone.

The drinks were still being tossed back, but plying folks with food was keeping outright drunkenness at bay. Wrinkling her forehead Brihanna wondered did she have enough food, then decided not to worry about it. That's what 24-hour delivery places where for. She continued chatting and kept a general eye on everything. Brihanna had made a blanket statement once everyone arrived, telling people to feel free and help themselves to food, drinks, etc.

This party was ninety percent self-serve and as the night progressed everyone took that to heart. People flowed from space to space, taking turns at spades while video games dominated the basement. Impromptu conversations popped up in the kitchen as folks were getting food, while some moved to the den for a little more privacy. But the later it got meant the tipsier everyone finally became.

She knew because the laughter rose in volume, not to mention the flirting and jokes increased. Everything was *more* now, from voices to gestures. All of this was good, as the goal of giving everyone a safe place to let loose had been accomplished. It was climbing towards eleven when Brihanna went looking for Danielle. She had sent her to get more cups out the den, but that was over 10 minutes ago. Going inside, the red cups were just where she had left them, on the floor by the bookcase.

Picking up the bag, Brihanna was about to leave when she saw a foot sticking out from the other side of the case. Recognizing Danielle's purple pants, she walked forward concerned, thinking maybe she wasn't feeling well.

"Hey girl, are you okay..." Trailing off as she saw Danielle jerk back from Darrell's lips.

"Uh, hey Bri." Danielle hurriedly buttoned up her shirt. "Sorry I took so long. I was just..."

"Letting my cousin check your tonsils. I get it." Brihanna shoved the cups in her direction. "Can you take these out, people are waiting."

"Yeah, sure."

Brihanna waited until Danielle made her escape. "Really Dare?"

"Don't start Bri. And don't go cock-blocking either."

"I'm not blocking!"

After shouting that out, they glared at each other. Darrell was the first to break.

"Seems to me like you have a problem, which I don't understand. It's only adults in this house tonight."

"I know that. I just don't want you taking advantage of her. She had a breakup not long ago."

"Exactly how long?"

"I don't know, almost three months."

"Bri...come on!" Darrell chuckled dryly. "We both know that's enough time for her not to be looking for breakup or revenge sex. I told you, your girl is always giving me the eye. Don't get mad at me for accepting what she was offering."

He had a point. Blowing out a breath of frustration, she held up her hands.

"Okay fine, whatever. I'll pretend like I never saw this and forget about it."

Snapping around and marching off, she was muttering under her breath. *Jeezus! The damn man can't keep his pants on for the duration of a house party.* And that was the start of the night getting a *smidge* out of control. When she got to the living room it was just in time to see Julian making an announcement.

"Hey! Let's play a game together." She held up a drawstring backpack. "I brought Twister!"

Among the scoffing, there were giggles too. Surprisingly, there were quite a few people in agreement. And before Brihanna knew it, the folks who still had their shoes on were taking them off. Then a few of the guys were pushing back the table and the furniture.

Devon saddled up to her and loudly whispered, "Dang Bri, I didn't know you were going to be throwing a freaky party. I would have brought my supplies."

"Eww, and it's not *that* kind of party."

"Not yet at least. Watch."

Laughing drunkenly, he winked at her, then declared he wanted to play first.

The game could only play four people at a time. They started by forming teams of two, one male and one female, facing off across the mat from the other. She took the first turn being the spinner. It was fun, and people were falling and cackling including herself. Almost no one was able to keep their balance long and the awkward positions had a few women and men flushed. Not unexpected with people being drunk and jittery on junk food.

It also wasn't long before Brihanna saw what Devon had hinted at. As the rounds continued, you saw some sly looks, and suggestive comments thrown around. In fact, what she noticed was that sneaky Julian usually made sure she was sharing the board with Lawrence. And each time she was taking too much damn pleasure at withering all over Brihanna's man, like she was doing right now.

"That bitch."

"Huh? What did you say Bri?"

Tina was standing next to her in the milling crowd waiting to take their turn.

"I said *that's rich*, to something Lucus said."

The man in question was standing on her other side and hadn't said a word. He was currently hugged up with his boo. Tina who hadn't gone easy on the drinks, accepted her lie and went back to egging everyone on. Two rounds later when Teresa fell heavily on her elbow crying out in pain, Brihanna decided it was a good time to halt this mess.

"Alright, alright. I think that's enough of this game." She watched Matthew help his wife from the floor. "You guys are drunk, not that I'm complaining, that was sorta the purpose of this party. But why don't we play Taboo instead? Less chance of injury."

"Sounds good to me." Samantha agreed, flopping down to the mat from the position she was still holding. "I'm too tired to keep doing this. I'm a desk jockey and so out of shape."

It broke up naturally after that, as folks used the time it took her to set up the other game to eat, drink and make bathroom runs. Soon enough they were all gathered in the living room again. Brihanna snagged a spot on the sofa and was hugged up under Lawrence. Not only to make a point, but it felt good to be in his arms for a moment.

They hadn't spent much time with each other tonight, both busy entertaining their various guest and seeing to the party needs. He had made sure to interact with everyone the same as she did. This game did the trick of settling everyone down a notch or two and got the spirit of competition going as they divided into two big groups to play it. Time flew, and the act of mostly sitting down had the desired effect of letting alcohol finally make people sleepy. It was a quarter to two when Matthew and Teresa broadcast they had just put in for a Lyft.

"Dang, hate to see you guys go, but I get it." Brihanna stood. "Don't forget to take anything you brought home, especially the drinks."

That was the start of the party wrapping up. Everyone started to say their good-byes to those leaving, as others got their belongings together. Malcolm and Brenda then Lucus and Valeria all left in the next thirty minutes. Brihanna noticed Julian hadn't expressed any plans to go home and that wasn't sitting well with her. When she was straightening up the kitchen, the devious little heifer walked in.

"Hey, I wanted to say great party!"

"Thanks, throwing it was Lawrence's idea."

"But we all know who did the heavy lifting for it. You put together a good time."

"Thanks."

Brihanna didn't have much else to say. She had tried talking to the woman several times tonight, but Julian mostly ignored her. But now she was all up in Brihanna's face.

When Julian came closer, Brihanna leaned back against the sink and waited to see what the snake did next.

"Do you mind if I'm honest with you Bri."

"I prefer *you* call me Brihanna, and by all means, be honest."

"I came for two reasons tonight. One to see how Lawrence lives. We hang out in groups every once in a while, but he can be a little private."

"And two?"

"I wanted to see what kind of woman had snagged him."

"Oh *really?*" Okay...what the fuck?

"Yeah. When he was a supervisor at our company, pretty much *all* the females in the department had a crush on him. He was cool, fair and really knew his shit. Let's be honest, he's cute as hell too."

"Mmmm." Brihanna was going to allow this chick to dig herself a hole.

"Then there's something mysterious about him. Like you just know he has some hidden sides to him."

"You don't say..."

"I can just tell." Julian smiled. "I've never seen him so loose like he is tonight. I mean he's fun when we hang, but not like this."

"You have no clue how wild he can be." And bitch you never will.

Julian's mouth twisted a little while she looked Brihanna up and down a couple of times.

"I guess I can see why he picked you. We all thought he wasn't into women who worked in tech, as he never went for any of us. But maybe he wanted more of a creative like you. You seem smart and quirky, kinda outgoing. I can see why he would find the combination attractive."

Did this woman just call her quirky? That was Brihanna's last button and the bitch just pushed it.

"You know what *I* can see Julian?" Brihanna started walking forward, forcing the other woman back towards the kitchen doorway.

"I see that it's time for you to call an Uber."

"What?" The inebriated woman wasn't catching on. "No, I planned to spend the night."

"Not happening," Brihanna gave her a look so cold it had Julian's eyes widening with the realization she was seconds from things getting physical. "Your plans changed, you'll be going home *now*."

Brihanna glanced up to where she had noticed Devon watching her.

"Dev, if you haven't gotten your car yet, do you mind getting an Uber X? It's lucky that she lives out in Oak Park too. You wouldn't mind making sure she got home safe?"

"Nope, not at all," Devon answered instantly. His face tight, having overheard part of the conversation.

"I...I couldn't..."

"You *will*. I'm sure my cousin feels the same way about you as I do. That he wants to make sure you *leave* here safe."

"Absolutely." Dev co-signed. "You don't want to take a chance...and get hurt."

Just then Samantha walked by and Brihanna waved her closer.

"Hey, cancel your car, Dev is getting a group ride. You're close to here and they can drop you off first and don't argue. With as much as you drank, I don't feel comfortable sending you home with a stranger alone."

"Okaay. I don't care how I get home, as long as I get there."

Samantha staggered off and Brihanna turned back to Devon.

"I know this might get expensive, but I'll pay-"

"Not another word about it Bri, I got your back." He glanced at Julian. "It will be money well spent.

When he turned and walked off, Julian tried to rush out the kitchen as well. But Brihanna snagged her wrist before she could escape.

"Can't *honestly* say it's been nice meeting you. Say your good-byes, especially to Lawrence...get your shit and get out."

Chapter Twenty-Three

May wasn't looking good, weather wise at least. It had been much cooler than normal for this time of year, but Brihanna was okay with that. The hot muggy days of summer would hit Michigan soon enough. Still, she was relieved that the day of the Royal Oak Wine Stroll ended up being mid-seventies, sunny, and with a nice breeze. They parked around twelve fifteen and immediately made their way to the check-in station to get their wristbands.

It had been a couple years since she last came. This year, eighteen places were listed as participating. What she liked about this event was you had to walk around, and all participating places gave you appetizers along with wine, which helped keep folks from being drunk off their asses. Plus, there were tons of restaurants you could have a full meal at if you chose to. The cherry on top for her was that a portion of the ticket sales went to local Boys & Girls Clubs.

The crowds were thick as usual even this early, which annoyed Brihanna because she was determined to hit every stop this year. Waits outside the more popular places could be awhile. Lawrence suggested they hit all the ones with little to no wait, then circle back around. It sounded like a plan so that's what they set out to do.

They got lucky and got into Bigalora right away and had a Baia Rosecco with a taste of white pizza topped with spicy, smoked eggplant. Not a combination she would have thought of, but that was why this event was so great. At Jolly

Pumpkin, they tasted Powers Cabernet Sauvignon and Dynamite Chicken. It was freaking fantastic! Crispy fried bites smothered in the house made Yum Yum sauce.

Lawrence was taking one small sip out of her glass, forgoing having his own. Sometimes, he skipped even doing that. What neither of them skipped on, was trying the food. He always got his own plate and if it was something she didn't really like, he would finish hers off. What a difference a year made. Last year she was spending her free time with family, working or occasionally with friends, and thought herself satisfied. Never would she have imagined walking hand and hand down a crowded city block. Letting a man sip from her cup and hand sharing food. Brihanna was very pleased and happy with the changes in her life.

Speaking of her man, she hadn't told him about the skirmish with Julian. Figuring telling him *not* to hang out with a longtime friend that just happened to be a female, would reek of unfounded jealousy. What she did do, was the next time he mentioned having plans was ask him who all was going. When he mentioned Julian's name Brihanna had gone with him. The look of shock on Julian's face would have been funny if Brihanna didn't feel like slapping the chick.

"Surprise, surprise!" Brihanna had shouted out as she sat down. Ken had been there as well, and the woman had been quiet the entire night. Probably because anytime the men weren't paying attention, Brihanna sent her a look that said, "Wait until I get you alone." Conveniently, Julian made up an excuse to leave shortly after the main course. Brihanna intended to be anywhere that heifer was, though her name hadn't been mentioned since that night.

Their relationship was solid, better than ever. Brihanna was soaking it all up, like this outing today. They hit a few more places before ending up at Tom's Oyster Bar. She had been in the mood for something sweet and they were offering Carrelet d'Estuaire Rosé with lemon bars. Fairly close by was Bar Louie, where Lawrence challenged her to taste the flash fried calamari. Holding her nose, she quickly chewed and swallowed a two-inch piece. Downing the entire glass of Whitehaven Sauvignon Blanc while Lawrence laughed uproariously at her.

Not that she hadn't been finishing her other glasses because she had, just a bit slower. After all, most places gave half of what a normal glass of wine would be, though she was surprised at how many were handing out full servings too. Thankfully, the white bean chicken chili at Oak City Grille erased any memory of squid on her palate. They followed up the tasty chili with Italian sausage, peppers and onions in zesty marinara from Rock on Third. By this time she was getting full, Lawrence wasn't. He said if he'd known about how much food they gave, he would have come years ago.

They were on their return loop and hit three other places that had been too crowded beforehand. Brihanna passed on the food at each and enjoyed her drinks instead. Finally, they were hitting the last place on the list.

"*I did it, I did it, I did it!*" Brihanna was jumping up and down as 526 Main came within sight.

"Just in time too." Lawrence mumbled.

Brihanna was drunk, there was no doubt about it. Lawrence had gone from holding her hand to wrapping his arm around her shoulders, mainly to help steer her through the crowd. Brihanna had started getting unsteady on her feet about three stops back. Since they were almost done he hadn't said anything, he was driving and she was close to accomplishing her goal of visiting every stop. He didn't mind watching out for her for an evening.

Lawrence didn't care in general that she was letting loose and having a good time. She wasn't obnoxious, but was getting a little extra exuberant. Like the fact she was now doing a quick running man as he opened the door. He tried not to laugh and encourage her, but he loved seeing her relaxed and happy. A minute after getting inside she turned, shoving her glass at his face.

"I'm good Bri." He said, pushing it away.

"Come *on* have your tiny sip!" She pouted.

"No. Why don't *you* have a tiny sip and put the rest down?"

"Nope, last place...I have to do it right."

Saying so she knocked back the entire glass before he could stop her.

"Ahhh, there I'm done!"

"Bri..." Lawrence just shook his head. "Okay, happy now? I think it's time to get you home."

"Not until I get my fried pickle."

Brihanna weaved through the light crowd to the snack table, grabbing up a plate. Turning around she almost ran into Lawrence's chest.

"How did you get here so fast? I left you on the other side of the room."

"I walked. How about we take your food to go?"

"Okay, okay." She pouted again, not really wanting the day to end.

As they made their way back to the door, she kept trying to shove food at his mouth."

"I don't want a pickle Bri."

"Well, I do."

Brihanna popped one into her mouth, then waved the other one around.

"Hey, I just thought about it. *You* have a pickle, but your pickle is *waayyy* bigger than this." She giggled gleefully. "I want your pickle, too."

That caused a few folks close by to chuckle and Lawrence quickly got them outside. The car was close, but apparently not close enough, as they were only halfway there when she started leaning heavily on him and complaining.

"Law, I don't feel so good. My stomach hurts and feels weird."

"Okay, we're almost there."

They made it but by then she was clutching her stomach.

"You probably just ate too much. Close your eyes and try to relax. We'll be home soon."

Lawrence buckled her in, since she was half curled up. It took a while to get even a block up the road as it was 4:30 and many people were leaving the event as it came to an end at five. By that time she had fallen into an uneasy sleep. His house was almost thirty minutes away, so he made a split decision to get her somewhere quick.

* * *

The lawn guys were running late, per the text apologizing for the delay. Robert hadn't been pressed about it, as long as it got done. The workers normally started when they arrived, but he thought maybe Liam wanted to speak with him. Which was why he opened the door without checking.

"Hey, sorry to just come over but Bri-"

"What the hell happened!" Robert didn't wait for an answer, snatching his sister from Lawrence's arms and storming to the living room couch.

"Brihanna, wake up." Robert shook her a little and only got a pained moan. Turning, he exclaimed. "What the hell did you do to her?"

"Nothing. She's just a little sick and a lot drunk."

"Why is everyone yelling?" Mika questioned coming into the room. Seeing Brihanna laid out she went straight for her.

"Because this asshole let Brihanna get drunk and now she's passed out." Robert yelled, standing to confront the other man.

"I didn't *let* her do anything, she's a grown ass woman. Which is something you all seem to forget in this damn family!"

Lawrence's patience was gone. He was worried about Brihanna, bringing her here for help. Instead, he barely got in the door before being attacked.

Brihanna moaned and that only set Robert off more, as he stepped into Lawrence's face.

"*You* are supposed to be her boyfriend, when you're with her it's your job to look out for her, *period*."

"I don't need you to tell me what my job is. I'm there to protect her, not stop her from living life. She's drunk, had too many different wines with a mashup of different foods. It's not the end of the fucking world. I don't go around trying to control her like your arrogant ass does."

"You need to watch your fucking mouth while talking to me, before you find yourself passed out next to her."

"Robert!" Brihanna snapped out, though her voice was weaker than normal. "Don't you dare hit him, or I'll get up and kick your ass."

Mika had helped her sit up, though she still leaned on the arm of the couch for support.

"You're too weak to do shit." Robert spat. "Which is why I'm pissed at this moron."

"It's not his fault, I insisted we-"

"Stay out of this Bri. Lay back down, I can handle your brother."

"Highly unlikely since you can't even handle her. Where the hell were you guys at drinking this much?"

"Where we were doesn't matter anymore since you didn't let me explain when I tried to. If your pompous, overacting ass really cared about your sister, you would be making sure she's okay instead of yelling at *me*."

Lawrence had had enough and continued his tirade.

"I *am* taking care of her, brought her somewhere close by so she could rest. Some place she could be sick in privacy, instead of the side of the fucking road. But *you* can't stand having someone in her life that she listens to besides you. I'm sick of your shit. You've been wanting to come at me since we met. So, do it. I'll show you firsthand how well I can protect Bri."

"No, I don't want you fighting!" Brihanna tried to get up but it didn't take much for Mika to hold her back.

"I told you to stay out of this!" Lawrence's voice lashed out like a whip though he didn't take his eyes off Robert.

"And *I* told you to watch your mouth. You don't talk to my sister like that."

Brihanna saw Robert shift to a stance and knew he was seconds from striking. "I swear I'll never forgive you if you hit him."

Brihanna was clammy with sweat, sick to her stomach and dizzy. She couldn't help the tears of frustration that rolled down her cheeks.

"You guys will kill each other!"

Robert watched as some emotion flashed across Lawrence's eyes before his face went stony and blank. Then he turned towards Brihanna with his hands up.

"You know what Brihanna, I'm out. I'll leave you here with your flawless brother."

"Lawrence, don't go." He didn't stop until she yelled out, "Law wait!"

But he didn't pause long before disappearing out of sight.

Chapter Twenty-Four

Brihanna didn't remember much after Lawrence stormed out, except yelling at Robert, crying and Mika trying to calm them both. After that, she started to get sick and they moved her to a spare bedroom where she spent the next few hours throwing up, dozing off and doing it all over again. When she woke up around nine p.m. it was to a dry mouth and an empty stomach.

Brihanna sulked to the kitchen for water and ignored Robert's offer to heat her up some food. Snapping at him that she wasn't talking to him, and just wanted to sleep before dragging herself back to bed. But once in the bedroom she texted Lawrence. He hadn't called or checked up on her, as if he had completely forgotten about her.

Bri-Bri: Hey, I'm sorry about today

It took a full ten minutes for anything to come back. She knew damn well he took his phone everywhere, and never went to bed this early.

Lawrence: Are you at home?
Bri-Bri: No, I got sick after you left. I'll go home in the morning

When she got nothing back, she tried again.

Bri-Bri Are you still mad at me?
Lawrence: I'm frustrated. I don't want to talk about this right now
Bri-Bri: Okay...maybe tomorrow?

One Click For Love

Lawrence: Maybe, get some rest

Brihanna's heart sank. The two had never had a real argument. Sure, they'd had what she called "tiffs", which were normally quickly squashed. They talked it out or came up with a compromise and moved on. Neither of them were big on drama. But now, because of a stupid mistake on her part, he barely wanted to talk to her. She didn't believe in crying willy-nilly because it accomplished nothing. But she gave into it anyway and quietly cried herself to sleep.

When she woke up around eight the next morning, it was to find Sheba sleeping on the pillow next to her. Reaching out a hand to pet the feline, Brihanna blinked her sticky eyes open. Not even wondering how the cat got in, they were resourceful creatures. The stuck-up feline actually sat half on her chest, depressing Brihanna more.

"Great, even you're showing me pity."

The cat just looked at her thoughtfully.

"I bet all that yelling scared you yesterday. Sorry about that. Blame your bullheaded daddy."

"I'm not that things daddy." Robert walked through the cracked door. "In fact, out Sheba."

Robert spoke firmly and pointed to the door. The cat blinked at him then slowly rose up, turned around and stretched with its behind towards his face. Before gracefully hopping down and strutting out the door, which Robert then closed.

"Damn cat."

"I like her better than I like you right now."

Bri scooted up to sit back against the headboard, while he leaned against the opposite wall with his arms crossed.

"Why are you mad at me?

"If you have to ask that question than you're bullheaded *and* stupid."

"My wife may have pointed out some things...I could have handled better." Robert admitted reluctantly. "I could have let him explain."

"You think? Jesus, *I* wanted to go to the wine stroll, *I* insisted on hitting every place and wouldn't leave until I did. You accused Lawrence of getting me fall down drunk."

"No, I accused him of allowing you to get that way in the first place."

"Allow? Do you even hear yourself? I've been over twenty-one for a long time, I can get pissy drunk every day of the week if I want."

"Damnit Bri! It was his job to look out for you, I stand by that."

"He did!" Flinging back the light cover she hopped out of bed.

"He was by my side the entire time. It wasn't like I was drunk or sick the entire day. I started feeling bad as we were leaving. He was taking care of me by bringing me here. Instead, *you* tried to fight the man! Now he's barely speaking to me."

"Sorry, not sorry. My first reaction will always be to protect you."

"You don't *ever*, do you hear me, *ever* have to protect me from Lawrence. Don't you get that?"

Robert shifted his feet, uneasy with the complete trust his sister had in this man and what it implied. So he shifted the focus to something else.

"What do you mean he's not speaking to you?"

"Just what I said. I texted him and he barely said anything. I get him being mad at *you*, but what did I do beside have a jackass as my brother?"

"Watch it, I'm not going to be too many more names."

Brihanna sneered. "Whatever. What, are you going to fight me too? Right about now I'd relish a chance to pop you one."

Robert rubbed his head, a headache was starting behind his eyes.

"I'm not going to fight you. But that might be why ass-wipe is upset. You wouldn't let him stand his ground."

"His name is *Lawrence*. You want me to respect you? Then stop disrespecting him, even if he isn't here. Got it?"

They locked eyes in a cold war of wills. It took a long moment before Brihanna received a slight nod from Robert, and that one thing made all her anger vanish.

Suddenly tired, Brihanna asked. "Now what do you mean by stand his ground?"

Robert shrugged. "Well you did undercut him."

"How?" Brihanna threw up her hands. "By not wanting my man and my brother who just happens to box, to fight?"

"Yeah, that. It's a pride thing. He felt he needed to defend his reputation as a man. You didn't let him. Win or lose he knew I would respect him more for trying."

"That is the most "male thinking" thing I have ever heard of." Brihanna laughed in disbelief at the stupidity of it all.

"And just for the record, I would have kicked his ass."

"That's the problem now. You men think you're invincible. That you're all Superman but you're not. Life would be so much simpler if men realized that."

"Ahh Brihanna, every man wants to feel like he's his woman's Superman. Even if it's not true, you have to let a man pretend every once in a while."

"I don't understand what you mean by that! Trust me...if you only knew. I let him be a man and I have *zero* problems with that."

By her blush Robert inferred she was talking about the bedroom. He had always shot straight with his sister and he wasn't going to stop now.

"Too much information Sis. And I wasn't talking about sex. I know we can be a bit much as a family and Lawrence isn't a fool, it's obvious how close we are. You keep trying to be a barrier between him and all the other men in your life."

"It's because I know you guys! I know how you can overreact, like yesterday."

"Yeah and I'll be doing it again if *anyone* brings my passed out baby sister to my house." He cut her off when she went to speak. "The main problem wasn't my behavior or even his, it was *yours*. Even ill, you didn't let him handle the situation, let him defend you *and* himself."

"What in the hell? So I should have just let you two come to blows?"

"Yes, if it came to that. You didn't trust that he could handle the situation. Which I don't understand. The man's been handling himself well so far. Yet, every time he's been around us, you've lied or evaded about him. Or outright tried to block him from us like at Thanksgiving and now this. Undermining him as a man and protector."

Brihanna rubbed her own aching head. Crying always gave her a headache and now this crap only added to it.

"I only did those things because it's *my* family and I felt like he shouldn't have to deal with you guys shit."

Brihanna was looking so forlorn, Robert tried cracking a joke.

"Why are you acting like we're some Mafia family who's going to jack him up on first sight? That's Mika's side. Admit it, you sprung him on us, so of course the cousins were going to be on guard meeting a guy you hadn't told them about. Someone you were making all these changes for. Cooking...wearing dresses, what did you expect?"

"How is this all my fault? And for the record I resent that remark. Why can't you see my changes as part of *my growth*? I am a woman, so why is wearing a dress once every couple of months a big deal? What is so crazy about me dressing up for special occasions? So-the-fuck what!

As for the cooking here's a shocker, I have a mouth and stomach, I need to eat too. There is nothing strange about wanting to learn something new. What I love about Lawrence is that he never, *ever* asked me to be anything I'm not. He never blinks at whatever I do, act, wear, etc. He understands, unlike you guys that I'm not one dimensional."

Brihanna started pacing, after seeing the hurt look flash across Robert's face at her last comment.

"Look, I know you guys aren't monsters. If I'm being honest, I tried to keep him from the family more for me. *I* didn't want to hear your mouths or Aunt D and Mama's endless questions. I didn't want everyone to scrutinize our relationship to death, while we were growing into it. I told both you and Dare early on I was dating someone, and you knew it was serious before Thanksgiving rolled around."

"Bullshit. I didn't even know the man's name, until you paraded him in my house, magically cooking meals for the negro! I doubt Darrell knew much more. I appreciate what you said and I'm relieved he likes you for who *you* are. We were wrong to think you were changing for anyone but yourself. Honestly though, the way your relationship was presented to us made the more obvious assumption seem correct."

"You're right and I've never apologized for that dinner. I'm sorry. He was just different from anyone else I'd dated. I *really* liked him. Robert, I was barely wrapping my mind around how important he was to me. I was afraid you wouldn't like him."

"Again, that's a problem. You're worried more about what we think than your man. I'd feel a little resentful too, if I felt I never measured up to the men in my woman's family."

Robert dusted off his pants before walking to the door. "You want my advice?"

"No." Brihanna said peevishly. Her brother just waited her out, until finally she half whined, "Of course I do!"

"You need to clear up Lawrence's place in your life, for both of your sakes. Let him know he's your only Superman. That he's not competing with me on that score. After all—I'm Batman."

It took Brihanna a few seconds before she burst out laughing, while he cracked a grin, then she was rushing to hug him tight.

"You are *sooo* corny but thank you. *I love you* and your twisted sense of humor even when you get on my nerves."

Robert squeezed her back.

"Love you too. But remind his ass if he hurts you, I will take him down."

Chapter Twenty-Five

Brihanna had no intention of relaying that last piece of Robert's advice. The goal was to make up, not deliver a threat—*men*. This was why she'd semi avoided them, too much damn testosterone. Able to keep down a breakfast of pancakes before leaving her brother's house around ten, her plan was to give Lawrence a few more hours to brood before she forced him to talk.

Brihanna was home less than an hour, before there was a knock on the door. Maybe Lawrence had beat her to the punch. That was her hope as she rushed to the door, only to see her mother. It was the first time Johanna had *ever* come over unannounced.

"Mika called you, didn't she?"

Brihanna knew Robert never would have. They had an unspoken rule to never worry their mother if it was something they could take care of without involving her.

"Don't be mad, she was just concerned."

"I'm not." Brihanna hugged her mother tight. "I'm really happy to see you right now."

Hugging her baby back, Johanna walked inside. "You're not going to cry are you?"

"No, I got that out of my system already."

"Good, I've always hated to see you cry. Do you want to talk about it? I'll make you some tea."

"Sure, but I can make the tea."

Johanna pressed her lips and shook her head, following Brihanna to the kitchen.

"I don't think so. Sit." She said sternly pointing her daughter to a chair. "From what I hear that's your problem now. You won't let anyone else do for you."

"What is that supposed to mean?"

"Exactly what I said. You won't let your man stand up for you and now you won't even let your own mama make you tea. You can't seem to let those that love you, *care* for you. Tend to you. Now sit down, and let me make you a damn cup of tea."

Brihanna clenched her teeth and watched as her mother rummaged around for what she needed. Mama rarely cursed unless she was really upset. Her mother's words reminded her of what Mika had said about cooking, that it was a way to show love.

"Sorry Mama, I just didn't want to put you through the trouble."

The water on the stove was already near boiling, so Johanna didn't say anything else, until she placed two cups of peppermint tea on the table.

"You've been doing that most of your life, you know. Not wanting to be a *bother*, you and your brother. You are *not* a burden to me or anyone else who loves you. I want you to get that through that thick skull of yours. You are forever trying to prove 'you can do it'. Running after the boys...trying not to be left behind."

"I had no idea that's how everyone thinks of me. What's so bad about being able to do things on your own? To pull your own weight?"

"No, that's how you see yourself. And it's nothing wrong with it. But why do *you* always need to carry the burden on your own? Particularly when you don't have to. Letting others help or shoulder the responsibility here and there doesn't mean you're weak. It shows you trust them. It makes them feel good that they can do for you. People who love you won't stop loving you because you *needed* them. You know that right?"

Johanna was truly upset with herself. She should have had this discussion with her daughter years ago.

"Of course I do. I've never doubted my family loves me."

"Hmmm." Johanna nodded once and decided to move on. "And Lawrence?"

Brihanna sighed heavily, "What about him?"

"I like him. And more importantly I can tell you do too."

"Mama, I do. Lawrence is...wonderful."

"How much damage do you think was done?" Johanna probed.

"I don't know, we've never had a real fight before. Hell, I don't even know what we're fighting about."

Johanna sat back flabbergasted.

"Wait a minute. Are you telling me you been with this man for a year and y'all haven't had a real fight? This proves my point Brihanna! What have you been doing? Being super easy going, nice and polite this whole time?"

"Of course not! I've been being myself. Not every couple has to fuss and fight all the time."

"No, they don't. But even the best of relationships have friction. You're no shrinking violet and neither is he from what I've seen and heard. Yet, not one real fight before this? I think you've been doing what you always do, automatically making sure there's no conflict, so there's no fear of rejection."

"You're way off base. That is not how our relationship works. We have a lot in common and happen to be on the same page most times. Why can't we just be two reasonable adults that don't get upset often?"

"Humph, you can be, I might be off....a little, but you should really think about what I said. Stop living in fear that people will leave if you make some noise in life. I know you may feel like that, with what your daddy did-"

"Mama!" Brihanna sprung up from the table. "Don't even go there."

Johanna got up much more slowly.

"Fine. I didn't mean to upset you. That was the opposite of what I came here for. I'll go, but with one last piece of advice. Don't wait long to talk to Lawrence. It's never a good thing to let men stew in their feelings."

* * *

Lawrence *was* stewing as Sunday afternoon came around. He knew he had been wrong not to check in with Brihanna yesterday after leaving. But he had been so pissed it had overshadowed his common sense, having allowed Robert to make him fighting mad. As soon as Robert questioned if he had hurt Brihanna, Lawrence wanted to knock the man's teeth down his throat. Only to become infuriated as she tried to protect him *again*. This habit she had of standing between him and her family hit too close to home. Reminding him of what happened with his mother.

One side of his mind knew it was a totally different situation. While the other part screamed at him that he wasn't able to protect someone else he cared about. He didn't want Brihanna to have to fight her family for him. He wanted to meet them head on and shield *her* from the negativity. Wanted to be her champion in every way. Lawrence didn't want any remnants of that young boy who couldn't prevent bad things from happening to someone he loved in his life anymore.

And yes he loved Brihanna, had been in love with her from the night they'd gone to Comic-Con. It was unreal that two months was all it took for him to fall in love, with a woman who had mischief sparkling from her eyes in a profile picture. Now look where love had gotten him? Sulking at home because that same woman thought he couldn't be trusted. When his phone pinged, he almost ignored it.

Bri-Bri: Hey...are you at home, I'd like to come by and talk
Lawrence: Yeah, but I don't want to talk to you today, give me a little space
Bri-Bri: That's too bad because I'm at the door

Lawrence looked at his phone annoyed, particularly when she followed it up with a knock. He was prepared to just ignore it until he got another text.

Bri-Bri: Don't leave your baby girl outside...

Fuck, she could be so damn stubborn at times. Even while he thought it, a smile wavered on his lips for the tenacity that was classic Bri. Opening up, he let her in. And damn if his eyes didn't drink her in like he hadn't seen her less than twenty-four hours ago.

"Sometimes you can be hardheaded Bri."

"It's not the first time I've been told that, and probably won't be the last. I thought we should talk."

"Fine, talk."

Making their way into the living room, neither chose to sit. Brihanna figured it was now or never. Wiping her hands on her jeans, she went for it.

"I'm sorry for getting wasted and sick yesterday and putting you in that position with my brother in the first place."

"I don't want your apology for getting sick. It happens, that wasn't an issue for me."

"Okay...then I'm sorry for the way my brother behaved, it was out of line and unacceptable. I've made that very clear to him."

"Damnit Bri! I don't want you apologizing for his actions either."

Brihanna thought she might scream a little. "Then what do you want? Why are you even mad?"

"Why? How about the fact that you don't trust me to handle the situation between me and your brother. Or that you think I can't control myself and would kill him."

"What? Maybe you were so angry you became hard of hearing. Even as out of it as I was, I remember clearly saying you would kill *each other*. I know you just as well as I know him. Neither one of you would have stopped with just a blow or two. You would have been a pair a pit bulls locked on each other."

Brihanna was pacing in agitation again.

"Why would I want either of the most important men in my life to be seriously injured? Especially over me and a stupid misunderstanding."

Lawrence snagged her arm as she crossed in front of him again. When he spoke next his voice was calmer.

"You...weren't scared that I'd lose control?"

"I've *never* been afraid of you in any way."

Brihanna remembered his unfounded fear. She thought it was silly but would never say so. He was no mindless would be killer, like the grieving sixteen-year-old version of himself he'd built up in his mind.

"It would have been a battle royale up in that house. Not to mention a hospital visit for you both. I was trying to save money on your health insurances, not to mention his home policy."

"Bri, this isn't funny." Lawrence refused to return her small grin. "Okay, I'll admit maybe I let my brain make some implications that weren't there. I went a little blank when I heard those words. But that doesn't change the fact that you tried to protect me instead of the other way around. Your brother was right in one thing. It's *my* job to protect you."

"Macho bullshit. Law, you don't need to climb a tower or punch my brother, even if he deserves it to be with me. I don't want you to physically fight for me. Furthermore, you shouldn't *have* to."

"Figuratively or literally, I don't care if I have to fight for you. Hell, I'll gladly go through your cousins, your brother, *whoever* to be with you. But you thought I couldn't defend you. That hurt me Bri."

"I never meant to hurt you, but you have it all wrong. I thought you *wouldn't,* not that you couldn't. That's a big difference."

Silence fell as they both were taken aback by her words.

"Why would you think that? I'd do anything for you Brihanna."

"Because why would you stay when my own father wouldn't? He walked out on a newborn, a whole family. I guess *I* was his tipping point. Just too much to deal with."

Oh God, her mother had been right. She had some deep subconscious issue about being abandoned.

"Oh Baby Girl, come here." Lawrence wrapped her in his arms, even as she tried to squirm away. "Your father was a complete and utter asshole. I have my faults but I'm not like him. I would never leave you high and dry, out the blue with no rhyme or reason."

Brihanna pulled backed, looking up at him, the corners of her eyes wet.

"But you did...when you walked out of my brother's house. Left me to be someone else's problem, and *that* hurt me."

"You're right and I am *so* sorry. I was livid and not thinking. But I promise you, that will never happen again. You know I've never acted like that before and I swear I won't next time. Can you forgive me for that?"

"If you can forgive me, then I can forgive you. Let's give each other this one pass since it was extenuating circumstances. We can yell, fuss or fight until we work it out or even agree to shelve it, but no walking away. Okay?"

"Agreed. Bri, you need to know what your father did, what any friend, man or whoever might do in the future, it has nothing to do with you being lacking or a burden. It's about that person's integrity. Your father was a coward. Don't let anyone else's insecurities bleed into you. You are a dope, creative, special woman. Don't let *anyone* ever make you feel different."

"Thanks Law...I didn't think I had let it bother me until now. Like you said before, the things that shape us are weird and often don't make sense."

"No, they don't." Lawrence let out a deep breath and led them to the couch. Finally sitting and snuggling her across his lap.

"Are we good now? Do we both know where we went wrong?"

"I think so." Brihanna smiled ruefully. "I think having a big fight and making up is actually considered a milestone in a good relationship, or so I've been told. Though I don't want to make this a habit."

"Me either." He kissed her cheek. "I don't think either one of us is made for constant drama."

"Definitely not."

"For the record I would never want to come between you and your family." Lawrence softly stroked her hair. "But I want you to let me protect you. To be the main one who cares for you. You're so ready to do it on your own, as if you don't trust me to handle it."

"That's not true. Besides me not wanting you to fight my brother, when else have I tried to stop you?"

"Going outside at Thanksgiving for one."

"There were six of them and one of you. I didn't want you to even have to go through that caveman bullshit is more like it. You're a great guy and sue me for not wanting to let my family harass you. I didn't want you to feel like being with me was too much. And *yes,* we just went over why I have those feelings. But you knew they were out of line too. That's why you hid that stupid basketball game from me. I never would have known about it, if it wasn't for Mika."

"You got me. I didn't want you trying to talk me out of it, or even worse come and hold my hand on the damn court. It was a friendly game of ball-"

"Friendly my ass. Is that why you came home with a bad knee?"

Brihanna made a quick mental note that Mika had been right about not letting the men know they had attended.

"Believe it or not, it was a way for us all to pound our chests without actually fighting. A way for them to take my measure and vice versa. And before you say it, yes it's an idiotic guy thing. Also, don't act like you tell me everything. What about that whole thing with Julian?"

"What?" Uh oh. "What are you talking about?"

"Come off it Bri. Devon called me a couple of days after the party and told me what happened."

"How did he even have your number?"

Lawrence laughed.

"It's Devon, I'm sure he has his ways. Anyway, because it *was* Devon, I didn't trust his warning that Julian was out to cause issues in our relationship. It could have easily been a ploy for him to start some shit. That's why I didn't say anything when she wanted to hang out. It wasn't a big deal since Ken would be there, then suddenly you were coming along. Even then I just couldn't see Julian being *that* bold or conniving. I've known her for years. The reason we became friends is because she was the only female who didn't throw out signals when I worked there."

"Well, she had you fooled real good."

"I see. After that awkward dinner I knew Devon hadn't been lying, that he was trying to do me a solid. Then a week later she wrote me a crazy ass email saying you hated her and how you were not the right type of woman for me. That you were jealous and needy. All things that are the exact opposite of your personality."

"I knew I should have hit her one good time in her eye, just once." Brihanna fumed.

"Don't worry, I did it figuratively for you. I told her you were the best thing to ever happen to me. That you were my perfect fit and everything I'd been waiting to find in a woman. I let her know that anyone who couldn't like you, couldn't be in my life because I didn't plan on you going anywhere. Then I told her not to contact me again."

"You did?"

Lawrence looked confused that she would be surprised.

"Of course. You come first Brihan-."

Brihanna caught his lips with hers before her name cleared it. Giving him a sweet, deep kiss of thanks and appreciation for his words.

"Lawrence, I love you." She could see his shock. "I didn't think we had to say it, you know? But I'm sorry if by not saying it I ever made you think you weren't important to me. That you didn't have a special place in my life, because you do. You're my Superman. You make me feel alive, free to be every phase of myself. I don't feel put in a box when I'm with you. I feel like you appreciate and see that...does that make sense?"

"It does and I *do* appreciate everything about you. I love you too Bri, and you're right we should have said it a long time ago. You are beautiful in how you accept yourself and others. Your fierceness and confidence is so damn sexy to me. It's a huge plus that goes along with your playful and loyal heart. Clicking on your profile was the best decision of my life."

Brihanna rested her head on his shoulder, inhaling the scent of her man, who was a *law* unto himself.

"That's because you're smart. And I'm the even smarter woman who replied. I know we'll hit a few bumps, but I'm excited about making our *own* rules for our unique journey."

Thank you for supporting African American Independent Authors. *If* you enjoyed this book, please consider leaving a REVIEW on the platform you bought the book on, Goodreads or BookBub. Reviews are an easy way you can help *any* author, and in particular Indies, get noticed. Reviews can be a one-liner or an in-depth (minus spoilers) overview of your thoughts or even just a positive "star" rating.

You can find a book club guide for

One Click For Love at www.TaylorMadeDaydreams.com

Author-Series Note

This is the completion of my first ever series! I have to say these characters took me for a ride. From the moment *Running Into You* magically morphed from a standalone to a series as soon as Mika spoke, to how Camden worked his way not only into Andrea's heart but mine too! Even though I wrote him, I was still screaming out "Where all the Cam's at?" Who could forget sexy, serious Robert? Honey, he could *Lorde* himself over me anytime. Unassuming Lawrence has me thinking about all the ways I can break the *"law"*, if you get my drift. They were romantic, caring, giving and all "man".

We can't forget my ladies who I hope you all found to be strong in different ways. Andrea is the serious, quintessential career woman, who just didn't think the ROI (return on investment) was big enough to bother with falling in love, until she threw all her plans out the window. Mika is the bold, confident, "I don't give a damn" woman that we all want to be. And like most of us she also has insecurities that she hides, until a stubborn man makes confronting her issues more than worth it. And Brihanna finally met a man that made her feel at home in her own skin. She learned that a woman doesn't lose her strength when she gives up a little control to someone she can trust. It actually gave her more power and proved she wouldn't lose herself by letting go once in a while.

As the books that launched my writing career these characters will always hold a special place in my heart. A sincere ***thank you*** to these characters who bugged me in my sleep and while I was writing their counterparts' books. I hope I did your stories proud!

Readers, you *may* end up hearing from those sexy, funny and naughty cousins of Robert's down the road...time will tell.

I really enjoyed them all! Thank you for taking this journey with me!

Taylor Love

•

Join Us For The Next Book

"Vacation Love Series"

Lovers Hiatus

Her vacation timeshare has a "tiny" problem. There's a grumpy, *naked* man in her bed.

Janae Williams has taken a sabbatical to finish her first stand-alone research book. All she needs is a couple of months of privacy to get her life together. Janae eagerly accepts when a colleague offers the use of his timeshare. She figures a remote cabin in the Upper Peninsula of Michigan is just the ticket. There's just one problem, the grumpy *and* naked man in her bed who refuses to leave! Damond is bad-tempered, stubborn and rude. It's guaranteed he's going to ruin her concentration. Even worse, he seems to be scrambling her brain with lust!

By Taylor Love

About the Author

Taylor Love is a Michigan author. An avid reader since she was a young girl, she gained a love of writing as well. Her hope is to share Sexy-Modern-Romances that mainly showcase African American couples in a positive, real, yet uplifting light! Making *romance* for all women a reality. She loves to read a variety of genres and hopes over time to expand her writing among several of them. She is a lover of learning a "little bit" about many things. May her imagination bring readers a few hours of enjoyment!

Taylor Love Books

Instant Chemistry Series

Running Into You

Not My Type

One Click For Love

Instant Chemistry Shorts

Cam & Andrea-New Year's Eve

Cam & Andrea-Don't Forget What You Have At Home

Robert & Mika-Weekend With The Lordes

Vacation Love Series

Crashing In On Love

Stay In Touch!

Facebook-
https://www.facebook.com/TaylorMadeDayDreams/
Author Newsletter-(No Spam-2 a month tops!)
http://eepurl.com/duB-Fn

Twitter- https://twitter.com/TaylorLoveWrite
Instagram-
https://www.instagram.com/taylorlovewriter/

BookBub-
https://www.bookbub.com/profile/taylor-love?list=author_books